She managed a brittle smile. "You want to be my friend and my boss?"

One of Taylor's eyebrows lifted. "Technically, I won't be your boss because you'll be the only one on the team working independently of the others and not under my direct supervision. However, I'll always make myself available to you if you need to talk about something."

Sonja chided herself for misinterpreting his motives. Maybe it was because she was his sister's friend that he didn't want any romantic entanglement. Besides, he'd warned Viola about attempting to set him up with her friends, and for Sonja she thought of it as a win-win. Not only would she add the restoration project to her résumé, but she would also interact with a man with whom she would have an ongoing no-pressure friendship.

She extended her right hand. "All right. Friends."

Taylor took her hand and dropped a kiss on her fingers. "Friends." He released her hand. "Now, friend, it's time we head down to the cellar so you can see what's waiting for you."

Dear Reader,

I have written several series about families residing in Florida, New Mexico, New York, Pennsylvania, Virginia, Louisiana, South Carolina and West Virginia. Now it's time for New Jersey.

Bainbridge House is the theme of my latest miniseries, in which the central figure is a French-inspired château in North Jersey. The castle erected during the Gilded Age has been abandoned for more than a half century, and as decreed in the will of the last surviving Bainbridge, the responsibility of restoring the property to its original splendor falls to his adult children.

Taylor, the eldest of the five foster children who were subsequently adopted by Conrad and Elise Williamson, is the first to volunteer for the project. It is only when his sister recommends he hire her best friend, architectural historian Sonja Rios-Martin, that Taylor, a supermodel turned structural engineer, realizes he's ready to turn in his bachelor card for a future with the young divorcée.

However, Sonja's plans do not include marriage. She's focused on fulfilling her commitment to cataloging the contents of Bainbridge House to jump-start her aborted career and add to her résumé. If Sonja is hiding a secret, so is Taylor and another mysterious character living on the property.

A New Foundation is the first title in the Bainbridge House series, in which you will be introduced to the other Williamson siblings. With ties that bind them inexorably together as brothers and sister, they are given a second chance not only to be loved but to find their own personal happily-ever-afters.

Happy reading!

Rochelle Alers

A New Foundation

ROCHELLE ALERS

HARLEQUIN

SPECIAL
EDITION

ISBN-13: 978-1-335-40477-0

A New Foundation

Copyright © 2021 by Rochelle Alers

This edition published by arrangement with Harlequin Books S.A.

For questions and comments about the quality of this book, please contact us at CustomerService@Harlequin.com.

Harlequin Enterprises ULC
22 Adelaide St. West, 40th Floor
Toronto, Ontario M5H 4E3, Canada
www.Harlequin.com

Printed in U.S.A.

Recycling programs for this product may not exist in your area.

Since 1988, nationally bestselling author **Rochelle Alers** has written more than eighty books and short stories. She has earned numerous honors, including the Zora Neale Hurston Award, the Vivian Stephens Award for Excellence in Romance Writing and a Career Achievement Award from *RT Book Reviews*. She is a member of Zeta Phi Beta Sorority, Inc., Iota Theta Zeta Chapter. A full-time writer, she lives in a charming hamlet on Long Island. Rochelle can be contacted through her website, www.rochellealers.org.

Books by Rochelle Alers

Harlequin Special Edition

Bainbridge House

A New Foundation

Wickham Falls Weddings

Home to Wickham Falls
Her Wickham Falls SEAL
The Sheriff of Wickham Falls
Dealmaker, Heartbreaker
This Time for Keeps
Second-Chance Sweet Shop

American Heroes

Claiming the Captain's Baby
Twins for the Soldier
Sweet Dreams
Sweet Deception

Visit the Author Profile page
at Harlequin.com for more titles.

Thy wife shall be as a fruitful vine
by the sides of thine house: thy children
like olive plants round about thy table.
—*Psalms* 128:3

Chapter One

"Momma was really full of surprises today. I still can't believe she waited until today to tell us that she bought a condo in a gated community, listed the house with a Realtor, and now she plans to take a two-hundred-forty-five-day around-the-world cruise. But what really threw me for a loop was willing us a dilapidated property and expecting us to restore it."

Taylor Williamson met his sister's eyes for a millisecond before he shifted his gaze back to the road and the bumper-to-bumper traffic heading for the tunnel leading into New York. "Firstly, Mom is a widow and an empty nester, and that means she doesn't need a house with six bedrooms. And she'd always talked about taking an around-the-world cruise when Dad was alive, but she knew he would never go with her because his parents were killed during a boating accident."

"I'm aware of that, Taylor, but why didn't we know that Daddy had inherited a mansion he'd planned to restore once he retired?"

"That's something I can't answer, Viola."

"And when Momma asked if you would supervise the restoration of his ancestral home I couldn't believe you said yes."

Elise Williamson had waited until her children were all together at the same time to reveal the details of her late husband's will. Conrad Bainbridge Williamson had left her and their sons and daughter a mansion in northern New Jersey.

"I agreed because it's something both Mom and Dad wanted. And, don't forget I wasn't the only one to agree. Tariq said he was willing to get involved once he finished his postgraduate program, and then later fulfill his obligation at the horse farm. Even Joaquin is willing to become involved as the landscape architect. Only you and Patrick are the hold-outs."

"But that means you have to quit your position at the engineering firm where you've just been promoted to an assistant project supervisor."

A hint of a smile tugged at the corners of Taylor's mouth. "I know, but if I assume the responsibility of overseeing the restoration, then not only will I supervise my own team, I'll be working for the family." His mother had given him two steamer trunks filled with blueprints, floor plans, correspondence and documents linked to Bainbridge House. Conrad had stored the trunks in the attic of the farmhouse with the intent to review them once he retired.

"Right now, you're the only one in the family that has actually committed. There's no guarantee that Joaquin and Tariq won't change their minds a year or two from now."

Taylor wanted to ask Viola why she insisted on being a Negative Nelly. He really did not want to argue with his sister, not when he'd grown tired of her complaining that she wanted to run her own restaurant kitchen. As a professionally trained chef she had secured a position at an Upper East Side Michelin-starred restaurant. And if she did agree to come on board once the hundred-room mansion was restored to its original magnificence she would have the autonomy she'd craved since graduating culinary school. She would supervise her own staff at the family-owned business Taylor had planned to convert into a hotel and venue for weddings and private parties that could accommodate up to three hundred guests. It would take some time before the property would be fully restored, and while Taylor didn't want a firm commitment from Viola he did want her to consider it.

"I know a lot can happen in that time, but right now I have to believe they're willing to get involved."

There was more than a hint of confidence in his prediction.

His brothers Joaquin and Tariq seemed genuinely interested in becoming involved in the restoration of Bainbridge House, and Patrick had offered to oversee the financial component. He had worked for their father as a CPA after graduating college. Then he'd become involved with a woman whose father and uncles were winemakers. Patrick subsequently divided his time between working in their father's office and at a Long Island vineyard, and after a few years decided growing grapes and turning them into wine was his passion.

"We'll see," Viola replied, her voice skeptical. "What I don't understand is why did Momma wait until now to tell us about the abandoned property?"

Taylor knew he had to be truthful with his sister because it would eventually come out that he'd known what Elise Williamson was prepared to reveal once all of her children were together for the first time since the passing of her husband of forty-nine years. That had been the second week in January, and now it was late March and Easter Sunday.

It was a Williamson family tradition for everyone to get together at Easter. Conrad's death was unexpected because at seventy-four he hadn't exhibited any health issues. Elise said he'd complained of feeling tired and had gone to bed earlier than usual, and sometime during the night he'd died from what the medical examiner documented as natural causes.

From that time until now, Taylor had established a routine of sharing dinner with his mother the first Sunday of the month.

"Mom kind of hinted to me that she had some news that involved all five of us, and if we were amenable it would change our lives," Taylor admitted.

"Did she tell you that Daddy had inherited a huge old house sitting on over three hundred acres in North Jersey?"

Taylor stretched his right arm over the back of Viola's headrest when traffic came to a complete standstill. He'd wanted to leave earlier to get back to Connecticut before ten, but first he had to drop his sister off in Greenwich Village, and with the buildup of holiday traffic he estimated he'd probably make it home sometime around midnight.

"She did tell me a couple of months ago that Dad had left us some property, and he'd talked about restoring it once he retired. He'd gone so far as to file for permits and approval for variances to convert the property from residential to commercial. But we all know that golfing took precedence over everything."

After their father sold his private equity/venture capitalist company he'd hired a golf pro to teach him the game. The only time he wasn't on the green was when it rained or snowed.

"Since Daddy's gone and a developer wanted to buy the property, why wouldn't Mom sell it?"

Again Taylor met Viola's large hazel eyes, and he noticed the dark circles under the brilliant orbs.

He didn't know whether she wasn't getting enough sleep or she was putting in too many hours at the restaurant. "She told me when Dad updated his will he'd wanted her to keep the property in the family."

Viola bit her lip. "I don't want to sound callous, but there's nothing keeping her from not honoring a dead man's wishes."

Taylor removed his arm and ran a hand over cropped coarse hair. "Maybe when you've been married to a man for almost fifty years you might feel an obligation to honor his last wishes."

As soon as the words left his lips he saw a flush suffuse Viola's light brown complexion. Although they were brother and sister, they did not share DNA. In fact, none of the Williamson brothers and sister were biological siblings.

"You're right," she said, apologizing after a pause. "Maybe because you're closer to Momma than any of us, you know her better."

"I'm not any closer than you. I just get to see her more often."

"That's not what Patrick says. He claims you're Momma's favorite."

"I don't know why Patrick would say that when she has treated all of us the same. And if she did have a favorite it would be you because she always said she wanted a daughter."

Viola laughed. "Being the only girl with four brothers definitely has its advantages."

A special bond had developed between Conrad

and Elise Williamson's five foster children, and it had grown even stronger when they all stood together in the courtroom to make their adoption legal. That day was imprinted indelibly in Taylor's memory.

At six, he had been the couple's first foster child. A year later two-year-old Joaquin joined the family. He was nine when fourteen-month-old Viola became his foster sister and the darling of the family. The year he celebrated his tenth birthday eight-year-old Patrick and five-year-old Tariq became his third foster brothers. Elise had joked they would not get another sibling because the farmhouse in Belleville, New Jersey, had six bedrooms and seven baths, and she wanted everyone to have their own bedroom.

For Taylor, not having to share a bedroom or a bed with another child was something that had taken him a while to get used to. That, and having enough food to eat. There were times when he slept and woke that he feared the social worker would knock on the door and take him to another foster home, and when he verbalized this to his foster mother Elise had insisted he call her Mom promised he could live with her as long as he wanted.

Not knowing who his biological father was and losing his mother before he'd celebrated his third birthday and then going to live with his mother's sister, who took him in because it meant more money in her social services check, had emotionally scarred him as a child. As a preschooler he'd grown used to seeing his aunt's belly growing bigger whenever she'd become pregnant with another child, and her drunken binges where she would pass out while he and his cousins had to find whatever they could in the refrigerator to keep from starving.

Taylor's deprivation ended when his first-grade teacher contacted the school's social worker because she suspected he was being neglected. He'd worn the same clothes for a week and appeared undernourished. Child Protective Services became involved and he was placed in foster care. Unlike some children that were shuffled from one foster home to another he was lucky because he had been assigned to the home of Conrad and Elise Williamson. Unable to have children of their own they had decided to become foster parents. He didn't attend regular classes like most kids his age because as a former teacher Elise had decided to homeschool him. In the sprawling farmhouse, she'd turned a space in her library into a classroom, and by the time he was eight he was reading at a seventh-grade level.

"If you're serious about overseeing the restoration, then I know someone that may be able help you," Viola said.

"Who?"

"I have a friend who's an architectural historian, and when I saw the furnishings in the mansion I immediately thought of her. She's currently working at a Madison Avenue art gallery, and she has an uncanny gift for recognizing and authenticating antiques. In other words, she's an expert and a genius in her field."

Taylor knew Viola was right about the antiques in the French-inspired château known as the Bainbridge House. Many were stored on shelves in the mansion's cellar, while others were in ballrooms and bedroom suites. The property was set back off a private road, surrounded by ten-foot stone walls with a massive iron gate. An on-site caretaker had taken up residence in one of the half dozen guesthouses.

"I know I'm going to have everything appraised for insurance purposes," Taylor said.

"And I'm certain Sonja will be able to ascertain what is authentic and what is a reproduction." Reaching into the tote on the floor between her feet, Viola took out her cell phone. "I'm going to call her to ask if she's willing to help you out."

"I don't want to impose on her if she has a job."

"I don't believe it would be an imposition because she works part-time."

Taylor glanced at Viola as she tapped the number and then activated the speaker feature. The phone rang twice before being answered.

"Happy Easter."

"Thank you. Happy Easter to you, too, and your family. I hope I'm not calling at a bad time."

"No, not at all. What's up, Vi?"

"I'm calling because I want to know if you would be willing to appraise some items in a house that has been in my father's family since the 1880s."

"Where is it?"

"It's in north Jersey. I have you on speaker because I'm in the car with my brother who will be responsible for the restoration."

"How many pieces are you talking about?"

"A lot, Sonja. The house sits on three hundred acres and has more than a hundred rooms."

There was a noticeable silence until Sonja's voice filled the interior of the SUV again. "That sounds like quite a project."

Viola shared a smile with Taylor. "It is. Maybe you and Taylor can meet, and then he'll be able explain everything to you."

There came another pause. "Okay. I have to go into the gallery all this week because we're having an exhibition Friday night, but I'm free Saturday and Sunday."

"What if I make a reservation at the restaurant in Taylor's name for you to meet him Saturday night." Taylor nodded when Viola's eyebrows lifted questioningly.

"That sounds good. It isn't often that I get to eat at The Cellar."

Viola smiled. "I guess that settles it. How does seven work for you?"

"It works."

"Good. I'll give my brother your number so if something comes up he'll be able to contact you."

"Saturday at seven," Sonja confirmed.

"Thanks, Sonja."

"No, thank you, Viola. You know how excited I get whenever I'm approached about a new assignment."

"Even though I'll be in the kitchen, I'll make certain to come out and see you." Viola rang off and then turned to smile at Taylor. "That's one thing you can cross off your to-do list."

"I really appreciate that." And he did.

Viola took Taylor's phone off the console and programmed Sonja's number. "I think you're going to like Sonja. And don't get your nose out of joint, because I'm not trying to hook you up with her—she's currently not into dating," Viola said quickly.

Taylor stared straight ahead as traffic began moving again. He'd lost count of the number of times Viola had attempted to set him up with a few of her friends. The year before, he'd read her the riot act, and she finally took the hint that he'd never had a problem asking a woman out. But he hadn't been in a relationship for a while—not since he'd dated an attorney exclusively until she decided to reconcile with her ex-husband.

"She sounds like someone I could get along with."

"You two are like bookends."

"Why would you say that?" Taylor asked Viola.

"Both of you are laser focused on your careers."

Taylor wanted to tell Viola that he'd had to make up for the five years when he'd dropped out of college before deciding to return to complete the courses he needed for his degree. He accelerated as he entered the tunnel and twenty minutes later he maneuvered up to the curb in front of the four-story apartment building along a tree-lined street in the West Village. Viola lived in a two-bedroom apartment in a renovated building with a doorman and rented the extra bedroom to a nurse that worked the night shift at a local hospital.

Viola unbuckled her seat belt, leaned over and kissed Taylor's cheek. "Thanks for the ride."

He patted her short curly hair. "Anytime, kid."

"I'll try and see you when you come in Saturday."

"Don't stress yourself if you can't get out of the kitchen." Taylor had taken the train down from Connecticut and into Manhattan a week after Viola had been hired at the restaurant. He'd wanted to discover why the establishment had earned the prestigious Michelin star and was more than impressed with what he'd ordered. The Cellar opened for dinner Tuesday through Saturday, and reserving a table was highly recommended.

"Just send me a text when you arrive, and whenever I get a break I'll come out to see you."

Taylor knew it was useless to argue with Viola, because once she set her mind to something, she was like a dog with a bone. "Okay." Viola grasped the handles of her tote and opened the passenger-side door. He waited until she walked into the lobby of the building and then programmed the navigation app for the best route to Stamford, Connecticut.

During the drive he thought about how his supervisor would react to his resigning within weeks of getting a promotion. Not only would he leave the firm, but also he had to make plans to relocate from Connecticut to New Jersey. The decision wouldn't be an easy one because he liked his job, but when he had to weigh it against not leaving or undertaking a family project the latter won out. He owed everything that he'd become to Conrad and Elise Williamson and for Taylor it was family above all. He tapped the screen on the dashboard and activated the Bluetooth for his mother's number. She picked up after the first ring.

"I just got a text from Viola that you dropped her off."

Elise was overly protective when it came to Viola. Initially, she'd been apprehensive about her daughter living alone New York City, fearing she would become a crime statistic. "Mom, you're going to have to stop pressuring Viola to check in with you. She's not a child—she's a twenty-eight-year-old woman living and working in the city that is now her home."

"I know, Taylor, but I can't help it. You don't know how many times I've blamed myself for homeschooling all of you. Perhaps if I'd enrolled my children in traditional schools where they were able to interact with other kids or signed you up for sleepaway camp and had other kids for sleepovers, then I wouldn't be so overprotective."

Taylor did not remind his mother that he and his siblings did not have sleepovers because they had one another. "Don't beat up on yourself, Mom. You did a fantastic job raising us. Just try and ease up on Viola. I know you're selling the house, and I'd like you to ask your Realtor to find a rental for me within a ten-mile radius of Bainbridge House." Taylor estimated it would take at least two years for the main house suites and guesthouses to be completely refurbished, and he intended to make one of the guesthouses his permanent residence.

"You don't need a rental because you can live in my condo for as long as you want. I've already furnished it. I plan to live here until closing."

"Do you think you'll be able to sell the house before you leave for your cruise?"

"Hopefully, yes. I have another four months and the Realtor reassures me he will be able find a buyer by that time. If not, then I'll close it up, take the cruise and deal with selling it once I return."

The 5000-square-foot farmhouse built on four acres with an in-ground pool and tennis and basketball courts would be perfect for a large or extended family. It was where Taylor had learned to swim, shoot hoops and play tennis. He and his brothers and sister had not needed a day or sleepaway camp during the summer months when they cooked and played outdoors from sunrise to sunset. The Williamson kids agreed they'd had the best childhood possible. They had also grown up with pets ranging from dogs, cats, birds and fish, plus a family of rabbits that kept multiplying until Elise decided to give them to pet shops.

"Thanks for offering your condo. I recently got a notice for a lease renewal, so the timing is perfect." Before he vacated the apartment he would have to pack up the furnishings and ship them to a New Jersey storage facility.

"You don't have to thank me, Taylor. You know there isn't anything I wouldn't do for my children. When I see you next month I'll give you a set of keys and the remote device for the gate. I'll also put your name on the management list in case you're approached by security. Better yet, the next time you come down I'll take you to see my new home."

Although Elise had dropped hints about Bainbridge House, she had been completely mum when it came to her purchasing the two-bedroom unit in a gated community with amenities that included indoor and outdoor pools, tennis courts, an on-site concierge for laundry, dry cleaning, recreation center, supermarket and coffeeshop. Conrad's death had left Elise a very wealthy widow. He had also established a trust to restore Bainbridge House with the proceeds from the sale of his investment company totaling more than a half billion dollars.

"Okay. I'll talk to you later."

"I love you, Taylor."

"Love you, too, Mom." It didn't matter that she hadn't given birth to him—he couldn't have loved her more even if she had. She was soft-spoken, patient, affectionate and fiercely protective of her children. Elise, aware of the traumas her sons and daughter had experienced before being placed in foster care, made certain all had been in therapy, individually and as a family group. The sessions had allowed them to work through their unresolved issues while at the same time forming and tightening the bond as a family unit. This is not to say Taylor and his siblings didn't have their squabbles, but as they grew older they learned to settle their differences without spewing hateful words with the intent to hurt one another.

Taylor groaned under his breath when he saw the traffic signs indicating delays on the New York State Thruway. Slumping lower in the seat, he turned on the satellite radio, tuning it to a station featuring cool jazz. The melodious sound of a tenor sax filled the interior of the SUV as he recalled the events of the day. He had reunited with Joaquin and Patrick, who'd flown in together from California, and Tariq, who had driven up from Alabama earlier in the week.

Tariq was on spring break from Tuskegee University where he was enrolled in postgraduate courses in veterinary medicine and had planned to spend the time with their mother. Patrick and Joaquin would fly out from Newark International at the end of the week. Patrick had delayed his return to go over the trust their father had set up for the restoration project in which Conrad had named his accountant son the executor.

Elise was ecstatic once Taylor agreed to assume responsibility to restore her late husband's ancestral home to its original magnificence. He planned to focus on the exterior before the interiors. It wasn't only the château that needed work but also the guest cottages, vineyard, orchards, stables, formal gardens, a bridle path, and a nine-hole golf course all of which were in poor condition.

Taylor had been forthcoming with Viola when he told her Elise had dropped hints about inheriting property from her husband she'd wanted to share with her children. She'd finally revealed that not only was Bainbridge House listed in the National Register of Historic Places, but a trust had been established more than seventy years ago to cover property taxes and salaries for future generations of resident caretakers.

Taylor estimated it would take at least two years to completely renovate the house, barns and outbuildings, and hopefully by that time it would be ready to become a successful family enterprise.

Chapter Two

"Do you still want me to pick you up at nine?"

"Yes," Sonja told her cousin, estimating her dinner meeting with Taylor Williamson shouldn't go beyond two hours.

Sonja alighted from the car and made her way down the staircase to the below-the-street dining establishment that had operated once as a speakeasy during Prohibition. This would be her second time eating at The Cellar. The first had been two years ago when Viola was hired as an apprentice chef. The restaurant had just earned a Michelin star, and if it hadn't been for her friend setting up a reservation for her she would've had to wait three weeks for a table. The food, ambiance and professional waitstaff were exceptional.

If Viola hadn't asked her to meet her brother, Sonja knew she would've spent the day sleeping late and watching her favorite movie channel, because she'd just had the week from hell. It had taken more than a month for the gallery owners to decide what they wanted to exhibit after they'd purchased the contents of a home in the Hudson Valley during an estate sale. Their constant bickering had worn on Sonja's fragile nerves, and she'd found herself leaving the gallery several times a day to walk around the block. The indecisiveness ended when Sonja became the mediator and there was consensus to exhibit a limited collection of crystal and silver pieces. They had belonged to the descendants of a Dutch shipping merchant who had amassed a sizeable fortune when New York was still a British colony. His subsequent descendants continued the family passion for purchasing crystal and silver for generations.

The restaurant's solid oaken doors with stained glass insets opened, and she exchanged a smile with the maître d'. The slightly built man wearing all black inclined his head. "Good evening. Welcome to The Cellar."

"Thank you. I have a reservation for seven."

"Your name, miss."

"Martin. However, the reservation is under Taylor Williamson."

The maître d' beckoned to one of the hostesses at the podium. "Please show Ms. Martin to Mr. Williamson's table."

She followed the young woman into the dining room with round tables covered in white tablecloths, with seating for two, four or six. Lit votives, bud vases with fresh flowers, Tiffany-inspired sconces and gaslighted fireplaces created an ambience that was inviting and intimate. She savored the mouthwatering aroma of grilled meats from a tray carried by waiter balanced on one shoulder as he passed her.

The hostess stopped at a table at the same time a tall man rose to his feet. Sonja felt as if someone had caught her by the throat, cutting off her breath, when she recognized the man staring down at her. She had never met any of Viola's brothers so there was no way she would have been able to connect Taylor Williamson with T.E. Wills.

Recovering quickly, Sonja extended her hand and her voice. "Hello, T. E.—Sonja Rios-Martin," she said, introducing herself. He took her hand, cradling it gently in his much larger one.

"It's just Taylor now."

Taylor pulled out a chair, seating her. He lingered over her head and she inhaled the subtle scent of his cologne. Sonja curbed the urge to give him an eye roll when he retook his chair opposite her. T.E. Wills was to men's fashion what Tyson Beckford was to Ralph Lauren's Polo brand. His image had graced the covers of countless magazines while he'd also become a celebrity spokesperson for a men's cologne and a popular luxury automobile. Despite his public persona, very little was known about his private life.

It is was if the mystique had enhanced his popularity and marketability.

She met the large dark eyes with her own curious stare. His complexion reminded her of the color of autumn leaves that had turned a shade of brown much like black coffee with a splash of rich cream. To say her friend's brother was a beautiful man was truly an understatement. It was as if Michelangelo had carved David from onyx rather than marble and had been branded the Nubian Prince. Taylor's royal blue suit appeared to have been expressly tailored for his tall, slender physique. He looked and smelled delicious, and she wondered if he was wearing the cologne he'd been paid to endorse.

"Does it bother you if folks call you T.E. Wills?"

Taylor lowered his eyes. "No, because that is my past and that's something I can't erase."

A slight smile parted her lips. Modeling may have been his past, but Taylor still had the ability to elicit gawking. "Viola told me you're a structural engineer."

He gave her a direct stare again as the corners of his mouth lifted in what passed for a half smile. "I am. And she told me you're an architectural historian."

Sonja nodded, smiling. "That I am," she said proudly. "You design and build structures, while I write about the history of architecture, and help to restore and preserve historical buildings."

"What made you decide to become a historian?"

She was preempted from answering as a waiter approached the table. He handed Taylor a binder. "Would you like to order a cocktail before I take your dining selections?"

Taylor accepted the binder containing a listing of wines and liquors. He was glad for the man's interruption because it gave him time to concentrate on something other than his sister's friend. Everything about her screamed sophistication—the shoulder-length dark brown wavy hair framing her round face, barely there makeup highlighting her best features and the pearl studs in her ears that matched the single strand around her long, graceful neck. He'd noticed men staring at her when she'd passed their tables and he was no exception. He didn't know if it was the sensual sway of her hips as she walked, the way the vermilion sheath dress under a matching peplum jacket that hugged her curvy, petite body, or her full lips outlined in the same red shade. But it was her sexy mouth that had garnered his rapt attention. He knew staring at her was impolite, but it had taken all his self-control to lower his eyes.

Taylor glanced at the beverage selection before handing Sonja the binder. "Would you like me to order something for you from the bar?"

A beat passed. "Yes. I'd like a glass of Riesling."

He signaled for the waiter standing a comfortable distance away from the table. He ordered Sonja's Riesling and a merlot for himself. Taylor shifted his attention to Sonja, and he watched her as she studied the menu. He'd arrived at the restaurant earlier than his appointed time because he knew if he couldn't find a parking spot close to The Cellar he would be forced to park in an indoor garage nearly a half mile away.

Taylor always looked forward to coming into Manhattan, and whenever he spent time in the city he chided himself for giving up the apartment in a Brooklyn brownstone to move to Stamford once he'd secured a position with the Connecticut-based engineering and architectural firm. The alternative had been taking the subway to Grand Central Station and then the Metro North to Stamford, and in the end he decided moving would offset having to spend close to ninety minutes, barring delays, each way commuting to and from work.

He'd grown up in Belleville, New Jersey, and it wasn't until he was twelve that his father would occasionally take him into his Manhattan office. He would spend the time reading or staring out the skyscraper's windows at the New York City skyline. Then he'd been too intimidated by the number of yellow taxis and pedestrians crowding streets and sidewalks to leave the office unaccompanied.

After he'd been accepted as an incoming freshman at New York University, he had fallen in love with the city that exposed him to people and neighborhoods he'd seen on television or read about in books and magazines. He hadn't realized how cloistered his life had been up until that time.

"Do you come here often?" he asked Sonja as she studied her menu.

Her head popped up. "No. Whenever I eat out it's usually in my neighborhood."

"And where's that?"

"Inwood."

Taylor smiled. "Have you ever eaten at La Casa Del Mofongo?"

Sonja's smile matched his, bringing his gaze to linger on her straight, white teeth. He'd warned his sister not to attempt to hook him up with any of her gal friends; however, Sonja definitely could have been the exception. Everything about her demeanor radiated poise—an attribute he looked for in a woman he found interesting.

"More times than I can count. My aunt and uncle eat there several times a month." She paused. "So, how are you familiar with La Casa Del Mofongo?"

"I attended college with guys from different New York City neighborhoods, and on weekends we would take the subway uptown and occasionally into Brooklyn and Queens to eat at different restaurants. La Casa Del Mofongo became one of our favorites."

"I try to go on weekdays because it's always very crowded on weekends."

Taylor angled his head. "How long have you lived in Inwood?" Culturally diverse in Upper Manhattan,

Inwood was one of the most affordable neighborhoods in New York City's most expensive boroughs. The few times he'd eaten at the restaurant he'd thoroughly enjoyed the delicious Caribbean-inspired dishes and live Latin music.

"Not long."

When she did not indicate a timeline, Taylor decided to switch the conversation from personal to professional. "How was the showing at your gallery?"

Sonja's expression brightened. "It was incredibly successful. We managed to sell everything on display."

"What did you exhibit?"

"Silver and crystal pieces dating from 1625 to 1710."

"Is it difficult for you to identify pieces of different styles and periods?" Taylor asked.

Sonja gave him a steady stare. "Not really. For example Derby porcelain was mostly unmarked until circa 1780. After that time to present day there are nearly thirty marks. However, some early pieces were marked only by a model number."

Taylor angled his head, his eyes meeting Sonja's. "My family owns a late-nineteenth-century mansion that was abandoned in the 1960s when the last Bainbridge died at the age of ninety-four. My father was the last surviving direct descendant of the original owner. He inherited the property and had planned to restore it once he retired, but never got around to it."

"Vi sent me a text telling me your father had died, but I was in Europe and couldn't get a flight back to the States in time to attend the memorial service."

"Everything was done very quickly," Taylor explained. "My father had instructed my mother that he wanted to be cremated if he died before she did. He used to tease Mom that he would come back and haunt her if she had a wake where folks came and stared at him in a casket. However, she felt it was only right to host a memorial service for his friends and former employees shortly after following his passing."

A slight smile played at the corners of Sonja's mouth. "My dad is the complete opposite of yours. He already has a plot at Arlington National Cemetery with instructions that he wants to be buried with full military honors."

"Your father is in the military?"

"Was," Sonja corrected, smiling. "He's retired, and he and my mom live in a lakefront house in the Adirondack Mountains, where he spends most of his time boating and fishing. After thirty years of moving from base to base he claims it feels good to be in one place for more than a couple of years."

"Did you grow up a military brat?"

She nodded. "Yes. In fact, I was born in a hospital near Fort Campbell. At first I really didn't like moving so much when I'd just made friends with other kids on the base, but as I got older and we were transferred abroad a different world opened for me. My mother, who taught romance languages, would take my brother and me on holiday to Spain, Portugal, France and Italy, where we toured museums and medieval cities and soaked up the local culture. Keith, who is ten years older than me, hated it. He claimed he didn't see the sense in staring at statues and old paintings, and eventually stayed on the base with my father. Whenever we toured a medieval church, art gallery or museum I felt as if I'd been transported back in time. I was sixteen when I told my parents I wanted to study art history." Sonja held up a hand when Taylor opened his mouth. "And before you ask about my brother. He's followed in my father's footsteps and plans to become a lifer. We never know where he is because he's Special Forces and comes and goes like a specter. My sister-in-law says she's in a state of constant anxiety until he walks through the door after being away for weeks and sometimes months."

"It takes a special spouse to be married to an active duty soldier."

Sonja's eyebrows lifted slightly when Taylor said spouse rather than wife. Unknowingly, he had gone up exponentially on her approval scale. She'd married a man who had assigned specific gender roles for men and women, and it wasn't until she'd had enough years of being her husband's *little wife* that she finally filed for divorce.

"I agree. But now that she's the mother of twin boys, she has a welcome distraction."

A wide grin spread across Taylor's face. "So, you're an auntie."

"I prefer Titi Sonja to auntie."

"Should I assume you speak Spanish?"

She nodded again. "You assume right. I speak Spanish, Portuguese and Italian, and understand French, although I'm a little rusty when it comes to speaking it."

Taylor stared at something over her head. "I'm somewhat deficient when it comes to foreign languages." His gaze swung back to her. "My mother, who is fluent in French, taught all her children the language, but for me it did not come as easily as math and science. I managed to learn enough to read a French-language newspaper, but having a conversation was and still is definitely out of the question."

"If you don't speak it, then you'll lose the facility to have a conversation. Maybe languages came easy for me because my mother is Puerto Rican and my *abuela* insisted on speaking only Spanish in the home to her son and daughter. Mami said her mother always tuned the radio and television to Spanish-language stations."

Taylor gave Sonja a steady stare. "How did she learn English?"

"She grew up in West Harlem, but when she entered school for the first time she was fully bilingual. Years later she married her neighbor's brother."

"So, that's why you're Rios-Martin?"

Sonja laughed softly. "Yes. Mami is an avid

feminist and claimed she didn't want to give up her maiden name when she married, so she opted to hyphenate it."

"What would happen if you married?" Taylor asked. "Would you be Rios-Martin while adding your husband's last name?"

"I still would be Rios-Martin." Her refusal to change her name had become a source of contention between Sonja and her ex-husband. She may have given in to a lot of his demands, but she had remained adamant about not changing her name.

"Good for you. There's no reason you should give up your identity because of marriage. I know several career women who have opted to keep their maiden name."

Sonja noticed he'd said career women. Would he feel the same if she did not have a career? On the other hand, that was not her concern. Her association with Taylor, if she did help with the restoration, would be strictly business. She was now thirty-four and no longer the wide-eyed impressionable graduate student that had fallen under the mesmerizing spell of her worldly professor. Her mantra had become *once burned, twice shy*. And at this time in her life, her focus was on her career and not a relationship with a man.

"There were times when I felt jealous of Vi," Sonja said, hoping to divert the conversation away from the subject of marriage.

"Why?" Taylor asked.

"It was when she told me she grew up with four brothers. Mine was so much older than me. By the time I'd entered the first grade he was already a teenager, so I always felt like an only child."

"That's because we spoiled her. Every once in a while we let her win when we played board games. However, she was a natural when it came to swimming. Even though I was older and stronger than Viola, I rarely ever beat her swimming laps."

"It sounds as if you had a lot of fun growing up."

"I know I speak for my brothers and sister in saying we had the best childhood any kid could ask for. Did she tell you we were homeschooled?"

"Yes," Sonja confirmed. "I've tried imagining what it would be like to be homeschooled and having my mother as my teacher. She probably would've been harder on me than those in a traditional school setting. My teachers told her I could've been an exceptional student if I'd applied myself. For me it wasn't about making the honor roll but passing my courses. However, I did excel in languages, art and history."

"Even if you hadn't lived abroad, do you think you would've become an architectural historian?" Taylor asked.

"I would've studied art even if we'd stayed in the States."

"Do you think you would ever live abroad?" Taylor asked yet another question.

The seconds ticked while Sonja thought about

Taylor's question. There was a time when she'd wanted to leave the country of her birth and live in Italy to complete her graduate studies. Her personal life had been in shambles and she was experiencing an emotional crisis. She'd moved into her parents' retirement home, living there while her father awaited approval for his honorable discharge as a lieutenant colonel. It was her mother who had urged her to stay in the States and deal with her dilemma, because running away would not resolve her problem. Maria Rios-Martin had become her staunchest ally and protector as she went through a contentious divorce and was finally able to exorcise the man that sought to control her life.

"There was a time when I'd considered it," she said truthfully. "Why do you ask?"

Taylor gave her a long, penetrating stare. "I only ask because if you decide to become involved in the restoration project, then I'd like a commitment of at least a year, with an option renewal for an additional year."

"You sound very confident that I will accept the commission."

"I did say *if*. I would never assume anything, Sonja. Especially since you do have a job."

Although Sonja felt properly chastised, she tried to conceal it behind an impassive expression. "I won't be able to commit to anything until I see what I'll be responsible for."

"That's understandable," he countered quickly.

"Viola mentioned the house has more than one hundred rooms."

Taylor nodded. "Bainbridge House was built in 1883 and is listed on the National Register of Historic Places. The main house is designed like a French château with turreted towers and steep-pitched roofs. The outbuildings are tiled-roof cottages."

"Does it really sit on three hundred acres?"

"Yes. It's closer to three hundred fifty acres with overgrown gardens, neglected orchards, a vineyard, a nine-hole golf course and a bridle path. I have copies of blueprints for the house and the grounds. *If* you accept the commission, then I'll make copies for you."

Sonja's smile was dazzling. "You got me when you said French château. When can I see it?"

"Are you free tomorrow?"

"Yes."

"While you two were making plans to get together I decided to bring you your wine. I waylaid your waiter and decided to surprise you."

Sonja's head popped up at the same time as Taylor's. Viola stood over the table holding a tray with their beverage selections and a shot glass filled with an amber liquid. She was wearing chef's white, and her curly hair was concealed under a white bandanna.

Taylor was so entranced with his dining partner that he hadn't detected his sister's presence. Pushing back his chair, he stood and kissed her forehead. "Are you doing double duty as chef and server?" he teased.

Viola placed the wineglasses on the table and then picked up the shot glass. "No. I told Joseph to let me know when you were here and that gave me the excuse to leave the kitchen for a few minutes."

It wasn't often Taylor got to see Viola in what she called her *zone*: the restaurant. As a young girl she'd been drawn to cooking and the kitchen had become her favorite room in the farmhouse. "You've got a full house tonight."

"We're always busy on weekends. I probably won't get out of here until well after midnight. We seat our last customers at ten. I just wanted to say hello." She raised her glass, waiting for Taylor and Sonja to follow suit. Viola touched each wineglass with her own. "Here's to friends and family."

"Friends and family," Sonja and Taylor said in unison.

Viola tossed back her drink while her brother and her friend sipped their wine. She set the glass on the tray. "Sonja, we'll talk later."

Taylor waited until Viola had left before returning his attention to Sonja. "How long have you and Viola been friends?"

"We met a couple of summers ago at a Washington Square street fair. I'd overheard her haggling with a vendor selling pen-and-ink sketches. He cursed at me when I accused him of inflating his prices and that I knew an artist selling similar sketches that weren't overpriced. I told Sonja about a friend who owned a little art store near the South Street Seaport, and said if she was serious about pen-and-ink drawings then I would put in a good word for her. She asked me if I would go with her because she needed artwork to decorate her apartment's entryway. We went to the store and I helped her select what she liked. Afterward, we went to eat and wound up talking for hours. It was the beginning of what has become a wonderful friendship."

Taylor recalled the collage of framed pen-and-ink drawings lining the walls in his sister's apartment and had complimented her on her choice of artwork. "I'm glad you could help her out. By the way, there's an extensive collection of paintings at Bainbridge House. I have no idea what they are worth."

"That's why people hire experts. I'm really looking forward to seeing everything."

He heard confidence and not bravado in Sonja's pronouncement. "I don't think I'd have the patience to go through duplicate sets of china, silver, crystal, paintings and other knickknacks wealthy folks felt they needed to fill up every inch of space in a house. I wasn't aware my father owned the house until a week ago. My mother kept dropping hints after the reading of his will that he'd left her some property he wanted her to give to their kids, but it wasn't until I was able to see what she'd been talking about that I was completely overwhelmed with the enormity of it. Talk about sensory overload."

"That's because during the Gilded Age those with a higher concentration of wealth became more conspicuous. Art is divided into periods and the Bainbridge House falls between the Gilded Age and the Progressive Era in the 1890s." She paused. "What do you plan to do with it once it's fully restored?"

"I want to operate it as a hotel and wedding venue."

Sonja flashed a bright smile. "Long Island has the Oheka Castle, North Carolina the Biltmore House, and now New Jersey's Bainbridge House will once again become a premier estate in America."

Taylor's smile matched hers. "I like the sound of that. I'd like to pick you up around ten tomorrow morning. If that's not too early."

"It's not too early."

"I recommend you wear boots because it rained earlier this morning and the ground may still be a little muddy." When Sonja nodded, he continued, "Where should I pick you up?"

"I'll be in front of La Casa Del Mofongo."

All conversation about the Bainbridge House ended with the waiter's approach to request their dining selections. Sonja ordered a mixed-green salad with lardoons and vinaigrette, and an entrée of ricotta gnocchi with white truffle oil, while Taylor selected salad lyonnaise, veal Milanese and marinated asparagus spears.

The seconds ticked while Sonja took another sip

of wine, peering at him over the rim of the glass. "I like Vi's toast to friends and family."

Taylor nodded. "I like it, too." Not only did he want them to become friends, he also wanted to hire her as the architectural historian for the restoration project.

"I'd like you to answer one question for me."

He sobered. "What's that?"

"How much do you know about your father's ancestors?"

"Not much," he answered truthfully. "Dad was raised by an unmarried aunt after his parents were killed in a boating accident. He was twelve at the time, and he claimed his aunt resented having to take care of him because she never wanted children. He left home to attend college and never moved back. His parents had set up a trust fund for him, which he was able to control when he'd turned twenty-one."

"Once I research the history of Bainbridge House, I will let you know what I uncover on your family."

It was obvious Sonja was unaware that he and Viola had been adopted; otherwise, she would not have assumed that they'd claimed Bainbridge blood. Years ago, following their legal adoption, the Williamson siblings had pledged not to advertise that they did not share DNA and consciously neglected to reveal they were adopted. It did not matter they were a mixed-race family. They were brothers and sister, and their parents were Conrad and Elise Williamson.

Taylor had had no knowledge of Bainbridge House or of the family for which it had been named until

Easter Sunday, when Elise revealed that the property willed her by her late husband now belonged to her children for them to share equally. Bainbridge House and the land on which it sat made them instant multimillionaires. Taylor and the others agreed it wasn't about money but carrying out the wishes of the man who had provided them with love, protection and selfless support in helping them realize their dreams. Conrad was a businessman, but he had taken on the role of father seriously. Although he'd put in long hours at his office, he always made certain to spend weekends with his family.

"Do you have a timeline to complete the restoration?" Sonja asked.

"I'm projecting at least two years. I have a brother who is an architectural landscaper. He currently has commissions to design the grounds of several A-list actors' properties, but once he fulfills his obligations he'll be able to focus on the gardens at Bainbridge House."

Sonja's lips parted in a smile. "Are you saying it's going to be a family affair?"

"Yes." It was going to become a family affair. "Patrick promised his fiancée he would join her family's winemaking business once they are married. He's a CPA and will financially monitor every phase of the restoration remotely."

Dinner became a leisurely affair as Taylor listened to Sonja talk about the cities and countries she'd lived in and visited during her childhood. He was enchanted with her exuberance when she recalled the first time she saw the Mona Lisa and art masterpieces from the Renaissance. She admitted she'd been so enthralled with the Eternal City that more than once she'd considered moving to Rome to live. Their time together ended all too soon for Taylor when Sonja declined coffee and dessert saying she had to leave because someone was picking her up. He settled the bill, leaving a generous tip, and escorted her up to the street level.

"I see my ride across the street," Sonja said. "I'll see you tomorrow at ten."

"Okay. Get home safely."

He watched her walk across the street and get into the passenger seat of a late-model sedan. Viola said she wasn't into dating, but that did not mean the man sitting behind the wheel was someone his sister did not know about. Although he'd found himself attracted to Sonja, Taylor knew nothing would come of it. It was to be business and nothing but business between them. Waiting until the car with Sonja pulled away from the curb, he turned on his heel and walked the three blocks to where he'd parked his SUV.

What he did not want to admit to himself was that he'd spent a most pleasurable couple of hours with a woman who had unknowingly bewitched him with her beauty, poise and intelligence, and he looked forward to spending countless more hours with her if and when she signed on to the restoration project.

Chapter Three

Sonja walked into the kitchen in her aunt and uncle's apartment to brew a cup of coffee and was surprised to find both sitting at the table. They usually attended early-morning church service followed by brunch at one of their favorite neighborhood restaurants before returning home to watch either a sporting event or movie. In a month, her uncle would join a group of retired police and firefighters for Sunday afternoon baseball games in Central Park.

The table was littered with travel brochures, and her aunt was busy scrolling through travel sites on her laptop. Her uncle was a recent NYPD retired sergeant, while her aunt had retired the year before as an underwriter for a major insurance company.

"Have you guys finally decided where you want to go to celebrate your twenty-fifth wedding anniversary?" she asked as she removed a coffee pod from the carousel and popped it into the single-serve coffeemaker.

Her mother's brother shifted slightly on his chair, peering at her over a pair of reading glasses. "I still want to go to Alaska, while your *titi* keeps going on about Hawaii."

Opening the refrigerator, Sonja took out a container of creamer. "Why don't you compromise? You're going to be on the West Coast. You can spend a couple of weeks in Hawaii, and once you return to the mainland you can take a cruise up to Alaska. That way it's a win-win for you both."

Nelson Rios blew his niece an air kiss, then reached for his wife's hand. "What do you say, Mama? First Hawaii and then Alaska?"

Yolanda glared at Nelson. "Now, why didn't we think of that?"

Sonja winked at her aunt. She'd just turned sixty yet appeared at least ten years younger. There was just a sprinkling of gray in the neatly braided twists styled in a ponytail, while her nut-brown face was wrinkle-free which she attributed to good genes.

Sonja always felt Yolanda Clark was the perfect partner for her uncle after he lost his first wife during a hit-and-run, leaving him a grief-stricken widower and single father of an eight-year-old son. Nelson and Yolanda had dated off and on for more than a year

before he'd asked her to move in with him. She refused, reminding him it would send the wrong signal to his son. Nelson had confessed to Sonja that
marrying Yolanda was one of the best decisions he'd
ever made.

She'd filled the void and had become a wonderful mother for Jaime.

Her mother and uncle were born with red hair, a
recessive hair color they'd inherited from their great-
grandmother. Maria and Nelson were referred to re-
spectively as Red and Rusty by neighborhood kids,
and the nickname had followed Nelson through
adulthood. Many of his colleagues on the police force
still called him Rusty although the red strands had
faded to a shimmering silver.

It was Yolanda who had urged Sonja to move into
their spare bedroom six years ago after Jaime married his high school sweetheart. Her offer had come
at the right time: she'd left her husband, enrolled at
the Pratt Institute to concentrate on completing her
degree, while commuting between New York and
Boston to file and eventually finalize her divorce.
Although she'd volunteered a few times to pay them
rent for living in the apartment with panoramic views
of the Hudson River and the New Jersey Palisades,
her aunt and uncle rejected her offer with the recommendation she save her money to eventually purchase a house or condo.

Their suggestion had made her aware that she'd
gone from living with her parents to sharing a dorm

room with another college student and then with the
man who would become her husband. After she left
Hugh, Sonja had moved into her parents' retirement
home, wallowing in a morass of self-pity until she
shook off her lethargy with the intent of completing
her education. She'd applied and was accepted into
the Pratt Institute with the promise she would live in
Manhattan with her aunt and uncle until she graduated and secured employment.

She'd earned her degree and been hired to work
in the Madison Avenue art gallery, yet still did not
live alone. Sonja told Viola that she envied her because she'd grown up with four brothers, but what
she didn't say to her friend that she was jealous of
her independence. Viola had left her parents' home
to attend culinary school, and rather than return to
New Jersey she'd rented an apartment in the West
Village. Viola's tenure had been short-lived when
working for a few hotels, and then she found her
niche at The Cellar. Sonja's best friend, six years her
junior, had unknowingly become her role model for
what it meant to be an independent woman.

She cradled the mug with both hands. The weekend was her time to sleep in. It was only on a rare
occasion she got out of bed before noon. And when
she did it was to brush her teeth and take a leisurely
bath. Sweats were her favored attire, and after preparing something to eat or heating up leftovers, Sonja
left the apartment to visit the local nail salon for her
weekly mani-pedi. She always called the owner mid-

week to set up the appointment in order not to sit and wait for her favorite technician.

"I have to meet someone for a possible commission."

Yolanda powered down the laptop. "What kind of commission?"

"Cataloguing the contents of a New Jersey mansion."

"Where in New Jersey?" Nelson questioned.

"Somewhere in the northern part of the state. I'll let you know where once I get back."

"Are you going to accept it?" Yolanda asked.

"I don't know."

And Sonja *didn't* know. It was not as if she wasn't employed. The gallery owners paid her well, covered her health insurance and gave her a percentage of the final sale showings. If she did agree to assist Taylor Williamson with his restoration of Bainbridge House, it would have to be financially beneficial for her to leave the gallery.

"If you do accept it, you know you'll have to quit your position at the gallery," Nelson said.

"Before I make any decision I'll have to weigh my options."

Her options would include travel time, salary and benefits. Taylor had also mentioned he needed a one- and maybe even a two-year commitment from her. Yes, she thought. She had to weigh and examine all her options, because if she did assist in restoring Bainbridge House to its original magnificence, then she could add it to her résumé to secure similar commissions.

Sonja had to constantly remind herself that she wasn't married, didn't have children, and therefore she was free to come and go by her leave. She would celebrate her thirty-fifth birthday in November and decided it was time for her to map out what she wanted for the next decade. Living independently topped the list.

She finished her coffee, rinsed the mug and placed it on the top rack in the dishwasher. "I'm going to head out now because I have to meet someone at ten." Sonja estimated it would take her less than fifteen minutes to walk to 207th Street.

She had taken Taylor's recommendation to select footwear other than her favored ballet flats, which she wore to work, or running shoes when strolling around Inwood or Washington Heights. What she truly loved about living in Inwood was she could visit The Cloisters, a medieval-style museum devoted to medieval art and culture. She'd spend hours there viewing paintings and tapestries without having to travel to Europe.

Sonja pushed her sock-covered feet into a pair of well-worn leather boots, tied them and then slipped into a waist-length down-filled jacket. In keeping with the unpredictable fluctuating New York City weather, the unseasonably warm early spring temperatures had been replaced by a chill hovering just

above freezing. After picking up her cross-body bag
and camera case, she walked out of the apartment.

Taylor double-parked in front of the restaurant,
drumming impatient fingers on the steering wheel
while taking furtive glances in the rearview mirror
for a passing police cruiser. Sonja had asked him to
pick her up outside La Casa Del Mofongo when it
probably would've been easier to park near her apartment building.

*I'm not trying to hook you up with her—she's
currently not into dating.* Viola's pronouncement
came rushing back in vivid clarity. Had she meant
Sonja wasn't dating anyone because she was already
in a relationship? And was the man that had picked
her up outside The Cellar her boyfriend? Had she
wanted to avoid having to explain that she'd shared
dinner with another man?

Although he'd found Sonja attractive he knew
nothing would come from it even if she was unencumbered. She was his sister's friend as well as a
possible future employee, and Taylor did not believe
in mixing business with pleasure. He'd witnessed
firsthand how office romances imploded after a vol-
atile breakup.

After he'd told his family that he would oversee
the restoration project, it had taken Taylor five days
to compose his letter of resignation. Viola was right
when she'd reminded him that he'd recently been
promoted—something he'd wanted for more than

two years. Based on the recommendations of several of his college professors, he had been hired by a major Connecticut-based engineering and architectural company, and it had taken a number of large projects and five years before he was rewarded with a promotion and more responsibility.

He'd planned to stay on until the end of the month, and then reversed his decision. He sent a memo to the director of HR that he was leaving his position at the end of the workday and was utilizing more than three weeks of accrued vacation time to offset the mandated two-week resignation rule.

Taylor was now free to concentrate solely on his family's property.

Patrick had emailed him, requesting estimates for restoring and updating the main house and outbuildings, stables, barn, gardens and orchards, bridle path, golf course, and vineyard. Taylor had emptied one trunk, and it had taken an hour of sorting through personal correspondence, bills of lading and other paperwork before locating revised blueprints and surveys. It was then he discovered that Charles Garland Bainbridge had spent ten million dollars in 1883 to build the castle, and once the property was fully restored it would be worth more than one hundred and fifty million. Taylor had replied to Patrick's email with a promise to give him tentative numbers before the end of the month.

Patrick's email was a reminder that he had to interview and hire employees to begin work on the main house. Time was not of the essence to restore the stables because Tariq had another two years to complete his graduate studies and fulfill his obligation as one of the vets at a Kentucky horse farm. Joaquin also had professional obligations that would not free him up for more than a year. Taylor had decided not to put any pressure on Viola to leave The Cellar to become executive chef for Bainbridge House, or for Patrick to oversee Bainbridge Cellars. If they decided not to come around, then he would hire an experienced chef and vintner.

It was 9:50 a.m. when Taylor spied Sonja, wearing sunglasses. Jeans, pullover sweater, boots and jacket had replaced the body-hugging ensemble and sexy heels she'd worn the night before. And with her approach he noticed her bare face and hair styled in a ponytail. Yesterday she was the sophisticate, and today she could pass for a college coed. He exited the vehicle and opened the passenger-side door.

"Good morning."

Sonja smiled up at Taylor, who was towering over her. Without her four-inch heels, his height put her at disadvantage. She stood five-four in bare feet, and she estimated he was at least a foot taller.

"Good morning. Have you been waiting long?"

"Not too long. I give myself extra time when driving down, anticipating traffic delays on the Thruway."

Sonja did not have time to react when Taylor's

hands circled her waist, lifting her effortlessly and settling her on the leather seat of the late-model Infiniti QX80. She peered over her shoulder at the three rows of seating before fastening her seat belt. "Your car is gorgeous." She pretended interest in the SUV rather than Taylor Williamson. Fortunately for her, he wasn't able to see her lustful stare behind the lenses of the dark glasses. He was wearing the same cologne, but had exchanged the tailored suit for black jeans, an off-white cotton pullover and well-worn work boots. Dressed up or down, he had the ability to turn heads.

Taylor smiled as he slipped behind the wheel. "Thank you."

"It smells new."

"I bought it as a birthday gift to myself."

"When was your birthday?"

"November first."

Sonja went completely still. "You're kidding?"

Taylor checked his mirrors and then pulled out into traffic. "No. Why?"

"Because my birthday is November second."

Throwing back his head, Taylor laughed loudly. "What are the odds that we would almost share a birthday?"

She stared out the windshield. "What would be even more weird was if we were born during the same year."

"I'll be thirty-six in November."

"You have me by a year," Sonja admitted. "I'll be thirty-five."

"So, I'm a day and a year older than you." Taylor paused. "I'm curious to know if we like the same things."

"If you believe in astrology then we probably do."

"There's only one way to find out," he said cryptically.

Sonja turned to look at Taylor as he stopped for a red light and met his eyes. "How?"

"There's a pad and pen in the glove box. I'm going to mention certain categories, and you write down your favorite. Then you can give me your choices, and I'll let you know if I agree or disagree."

If Taylor was curious about her likes and dislikes, then she was equally curious about his. She'd told her aunt and uncle that she had to think about whether she was willing to leave the gallery, but during the walk from the apartment building to the restaurant to meet Taylor she had made her decision to accept his offer. After earning her MFA, she'd worked temporary jobs as a museum docent and a substitute art history teacher for an Upper West Side prep school. And when her tenure ended, she was left looking for future employment. She had discovered her current position when she saw a help-wanted sign in the window. She contacted the owners of the gallery and was hired on the spot when she was able to correctly identify every item on display. Now, after nearly two years, it was time for a change.

She retrieved the pad and pen. "I'm ready, Taylor."

"What genre of music do you like?"

Sonja jotted down her choice. The list grew with each interest. "Let's see if we're alike or polar opposites. We'll begin with music. I picked hip-hop and R & B."

"Cool jazz."

She put an *X* next to her choice. "Sports."

"Baseball."

"That's our first match," Sonja said, smiling. "How about books?"

"Legal thrillers."

"Romance or art," she countered. "But I have read John Grisham."

"Then, that should be a half match," Taylor argued quietly.

"Have you ever read a romance novel?"

"Yes. Viola is addicted to them, and one day I read one to see what the allure is. I must admit I enjoyed the book because the writer didn't treat the hero like a jerk. In fact, I really liked him, while I was pissed off that the heroine made him jump through hoops before she admitted she wanted to marry him."

"That's the genre, Taylor. It's boy meets girl, boy loses girl, and then boy finds girl and they live happily ever after."

"But all of the novels are the same."

"That's where you're wrong," Sonja countered. "The theme is the same because it's a genre, but the plots vary and the protagonists are different."

Taylor tapped the navigation screen displaying the programmed route. "Like the movies on the Hallmark Channel?"

She gave him an incredulous look. "For someone who is into legal thrillers, you know an awful lot about romance novels and the Hallmark Channel."

"That's because I'm the only one Viola could convince to sit and watch them with her. My brothers always found something to do whenever she asked them to join her."

"So, you're the good brother," she drawled.

Taylor smiled. "No. Currently, I'm the one living closest to her. Two of my brothers live in California and the other one is in Kentucky. Whenever I drive down to see my mother, I try and stop by Viola's apartment to hang out with her for a few hours, and her television is always tuned to the Hallmark Channel. What I don't understand is why they show Christmas-themed movies during the summer."

Sonja had no intention of getting into an exchange with Taylor about the channel that had become one of her favorites. "They feature them because viewers love Christmas anytime of the year," she said with a hint of finality.

"I'd like you to answer one question for me before we go to the next category."

"What's that?"

"Why do you read romance novels?"

The seconds ticked. "Well, for me it's the predictability. I know it's going to end happily for the hero and heroine."

"But it's fantasy, Sonja."

"It's not fantasy, Taylor, but escapism. For a few hours I'm able to escape into a place where two people will overcome the obstacles and conflicts threatening their happiness."

"So, it's not that you're living vicariously through the characters?"

"Not at all," she protested. "Even though I'm not married or in a relationship, that in no way translates into my identifying with fictional characters." She didn't see the smile tilting the corners of Taylor's mouth at the same time she glanced at the notations on the pad. "The next one on the list is color."

"I'm partial to blues and grays."

"That doesn't get a check because I prefer earth tones. What about art?" she asked.

"African masks. I have a collection of masks and paintings with masks."

A gasp of shock slipped past Sonja's lips. "That gets a double check. I've just begun collecting them. When I was in Venice earlier this year I bought one from an African street vendor to add to those worn at carnival. Where did you get your masks?"

"One of my former coworkers has a brother in Nigeria who is a sculptor, and I have bought a number of his pieces."

"I'd love to see your collection."

"Right now they're packed away, but perhaps one

of these days you'll get to see them. What's next?" Taylor asked.

"Favorite foods. I like Caribbean and Southern."

Taylor chuckled. "Again a double check."

"Favorite time of the year."

"Fall and winter."

Sonja angled her head. "That gets a half check because I like the change of seasons."

"Okay. I'll accept that. What's next?"

"Photography."

"Black and white," Taylor said.

"That's another check," Sonja confirmed.

"Favorite time of the day?"

"Late night."

"Bingo," Sonja drawled. She counted the number of checks. "It looks as if we are more compatible than not."

"That's good to know."

"And I agree, if we're going to be working together."

Taylor's fingers tightened on the steering wheel. He didn't know what had transpired in Sonja's life in less than twenty-four hours for her to hint about becoming a part of the restoration team he'd hoped to establish over the coming months. He'd also wanted to pump his fist in triumph when she'd revealed she wasn't married or in a relationship. He did not want to have to deal with a jealous or controlling husband or boyfriend.

"There's also something else we have in common."

"What's that?" Sonja asked.

"I noticed you brought a camera, and I also have one in the cargo area. There's so much to see that I know I won't be able to recall it all."

Sonja pressed her head against the headrest. "I've thought about what you've told me about Bainbridge House and I'm willing to accept your offer based on salary, benefits and perks."

Taylor had informed Patrick that he would assume the responsibility to establishing salaries based on an applicant's education, licensing and certification. The total restoration budget would support Taylor hiring the best tradespeople in the region.

"We'll discuss salary and bennies later. Do you have a valid driver's license?"

"Yes. Why?"

"I am willing to provide you with a leased car and put you up in a nearby hotel to cut down on the time you'd have to commute from Inwood to an area north of the Delaware Water Gap."

With wide eyes, Sonja gave him a lengthy look. "It's that far?"

"Yes. Bainbridge House was built close to the Dryden Kuser Natural Area known as the highest point in New Jersey."

"It sounds as if it's in the boonies."

"Not quite. There are a lot of small Jersey towns

in the area, and New York's Port Jervis is a short drive away."

"How long will take it us to drive from Inwood to Bainbridge House?"

"At least ninety minutes, barring traffic delays."

Sonja shook her head. "There's no way I want to spend three hours a day driving to and from work." She paused. "What about you, Taylor? Do you plan to commute from Connecticut?"

"No. I've already made plans to live in my mother's Sparta condo. It's about an hour's drive so that's manageable for me."

"What about your place in Stamford?"

"I'm not renewing my lease. I've arranged for a moving company to pack up everything and take it to a New Jersey storage facility."

"It appears you have all of your ducks in a row."

"I have to because I don't like surprises or chaos."

"Are you warning me that you're going to be a harsh taskmaster?"

A silence filled the vehicle for several seconds. "No. I don't yell or threaten, Sonja, and on a project, any foreman who does that will be terminated on the spot. As a new hire with my former employer I had a supervisor who was verbally abusive to everyone, and I swore once I was promoted to a supervisory position I'd never treat adults like recalcitrant children. The overall morale was so low and the construction site so toxic we'd talked about walking out en masse and quitting. It ended when word got back to a VP and the supervisor was fired. I was promoted as an assistant construction site supervisor. Unfortunately, my promotion came only a few months before my mother revealed she wanted us to restore the property, and it didn't go over well with some of my coworkers."

"They know you, Taylor, and are probably apprehensive as to who they would eventually get to replace you."

"You're probably right, but I can't dwell on it because it's my past."

Like your modeling career, Sonja mused. She marveled that it was so easy for him to dismiss his past while she was still struggling to deal with the events in her failed marriage. They were traumatic enough for her to reject any man who expressed an interest in her—and that included dating.

"Your position will be vastly different from the other workers."

She blinked slowly. "Why would you say that?"

"Because you'll be autonomous. You will be responsible for appraising every item in the mansion while deciding which architectural features should be repaired or replaced."

"I hope you're patient, because that means I'll have to go through every room in the house and give you a report."

"That's not going to pose a problem, Sonja. I've projected up to two years to restore the interior and exterior of the main house. I'd like to start work on the exterior before it gets too cold."

For the first time since she'd answered Viola's call, Sonja experienced an excitement that made her look forward to beginning a new artistic venture. Taylor unknowingly would assist her in becoming more independent once she moved to a hotel as he'd promised. She didn't have a problem sharing the apartment with her aunt and uncle, but at her age she should've been living alone. She'd dreamed of decorating her place and occasionally hosting little get-togethers for her friends, coworkers and family members. Hopefully, after she completed her commission to restore Bainbridge House, she would be able to concentrate on moving into a condo or co-operative.

She settled back against the leather seat and watched the passing landscape as Taylor followed the road signs leading to the Governor Mario Cuomo Bridge. It would be her first time crossing the new twin cable-stayed bridge spanning the Hudson River between Tarrytown and Nyack.

Living temporarily in a hotel and having a car at her disposal was a pleasantly unexpected perk.

"Cool jazz or R&B?"

Sonja knew Taylor was asking what she wanted to listen to. "Cool jazz."

He winked at her when she gave him a wide grin. "We'll listen to R&B on the return ride."

"Thank you, Taylor."

He shook his head. "I should be the one thanking you. You're going to make my job easier because I don't have to search for an appraiser. We have a tentative estimate that once the property is fully restored it will be worth one hundred-fifty million. But that doesn't consider the contents. You will be responsible for authenticating the value of silver, crystal, china, paintings and furnishings."

"It's going to take time to go through everything, but I promise to do my best to make Bainbridge House a showplace for the twenty-first century and beyond."

Chapter Four

Sonja hadn't realized she was holding her breath until she felt constriction in her chest forcing her to exhale. She was a sightseer, staring out the passenger-side window at the passing towns named McAfee, Sussex and Quarryville. She'd become more alert once Taylor maneuvered off the main road and onto a private one. A fading sign indicating the number of feet to Bainbridge House came into view as Taylor slowed and maneuvered into the hidden driveway. Age-old trees lining a cobblestone roadway were just beginning to display their spring yield, and she tried to imagine what they would look like during the height of summer.

Within minutes of hanging up after Viola's phone

call, Sonja had wondered about how the Williamsons were connected to the historical property. Were Viola's ancestors free people of color who had made a fortune before or following the Civil War and had purchased three hundred acres on which to build their mansion? She did not want to think of another possible scenario where a wealthy white man had fathered a child of color and had left him the property in his will. Sonja knew the questions would plague her until she was able to begin an intensive search on the Bainbridge family.

Taylor drove through a massive open iron gate and Sonja felt as she'd been transported back to a time in Europe where châteaus were country retreats for royals and nobility. A gasp escaped her when she got her first glimpse of Bainbridge House. The château was built on a hilltop overlooking a broad expanse of recently mowed green fields; soot and fading stones did little to lessen her enthusiasm to view the interiors. The authenticity of the design made her wonder if the château had been disassembled in Europe, transported to the States, and then rebuilt brick by brick.

Taylor stopped and cut off the engine in the circular driveway. "What do you think?"

Sonja removed her sunglasses, setting them on the console between the front seats, and then undid her seat belt. "I can see why you said you were overwhelmed. Bainbridge House is magnificent. It reminds of the castles in the Loire Valley. By the way, I noticed the grass has been cut."

"The caretaker keeps the grass from being over-grown." Taylor also unsnapped his belt. "Are you ready to see what's waiting for you?"

He had asked her if she was ready, but Sonja wasn't certain she actually was ready to take on what she assumed was a monumental project. She'd viewed and toured more châteaus, monasteries, cas-tles, museums and churches than she could count both as a child and an adult, and being a student of art, she never ceased to be awed by the exteriors, interiors and their contents. However, this was dif-ferent. This was to be the first time she would be responsible for cataloguing and managing artistic and cultural collections. She did not have the post-graduate degree to become a curator at a national museum; however, she did have knowledge of res-toration and art history.

She gave him a bright smile. "Yes."

Reaching for her camera, Sonja waited for Taylor to get out and come around to help her down. He'd rested his hand at the small of her back and then dropped it. "I called Dominic Shaw to let him know we were coming today to leave the gate open and air out several rooms on each floor of the house."

"He lives here year-round?"

"Yes. Mom says he calls her whenever he's going on vacation, and that means the property is left unat-tended. I informed him yesterday that I'd scheduled a security company to wire the house and the grounds because once the renovations begin work people will be coming and going at different times and days."

"I'm surprised it wasn't done before."

"So was I," Taylor admitted. "I'm guessing that because the house is off the beaten track and surrounded by high walls and a fence it hasn't become a target for vandals and trespassers. I'm certain folks in the area being aware that the property isn't abandoned also acts as a deterrent."

Sonja wanted to tell Taylor that walls, gates and resident caretakers were no match for those intent on burglarizing the house and taking off with valuable items that were irreplaceable. And if Charles Bainbridge had spent ten million dollars to build his home, she was certain he had spared no expense decorating it.

They mounted the half dozen steps to the front door, flanked by window boxes with overgrown ferns. Taylor opened the door, and Sonja followed him into an entrance hall with rooms branching to the right. Grit on the marble flooring made a crunching sound as she glanced up at curving twin staircases leading to the second story. A massive chandelier, covered with cobwebs, sat on a drop cloth in the middle of the expansive space.

She shivered slightly from the cool air filtering through open windows and decided not to take off her jacket. "This place is going to need a good cleaning, Taylor."

He nodded. "I'm waiting for a callback from a maintenance company to schedule a time for them to come in and clean the entire house. I don't want to bring them in until cameras are installed. And I really didn't want to bring you here until it was thoroughly cleaned. But I needed to know if you were willing to join the project because my brother Patrick is doing double duty as the restoration's CFO and working for his fiancée's uncle's Napa vineyard. He divides his time between California and Long Island. He's been sending me emails every day asking for figures so he can draw up a tentative payroll."

"Have you hired your team?"

"Not yet. I plan to hire an architect as project manager, while I'll continue to supervise the overall restoration. I've given also given Patrick the figures for the prevailing pay scale for architects, carpenters, plumbers, electricians and painters."

"Do you know how many workers you'll need?"

"No. I gave him an approximate number that can always be adjusted either up or down. Now I'm going take you upstairs to see several bedroom suites, and then we'll go downstairs to the cellar, where the collection of paintings, china, silver and crystal are stored."

There were many more questions Sonja wanted to ask Taylor but decided to wait. She wanted to know if he'd projected a date when he wanted to begin work because it would take time for him to interview and hire his team.

She climbed the staircase, noticing the worn carpeting on the stairs and on the second story hallway. There were several rooms stenciled with Water Closet on the doors. She stopped, opened the door and saw a narrow space with a commode and shower stall. Sonja entered the first bedroom suite on her right at the top of the staircase. Massive mahogany pieces made the space appear smaller than it actually was. The queen-size bed with a decoratively carved headboard and two bedside tables, an enormous armoire, overstuffed armchairs, a round table with four pull-up chairs, a woven rice container under a console, storage chest at the foot of the bed and a cushioned rocker under tall, narrow windows would have made her feel claustrophobic if she had been assigned to this bedroom.

"What do you think?" Taylor asked as he stood behind her.

"The mahogany pieces are exquisite, but less would be better." Raising her camera, Sonja took several shots of the furnishings.

He moved closer, his moist breath feathering over her ear. "Can you imagine getting up in the middle of the night without turning on the light while attempting to find your way to the door through this maze?"

Sonja couldn't help laughing. "No." She sobered. "What I like is the Caribbean influence in the mahogany carvings on the headboard and armoire. The console, which is in the French Regency style, has an intricate Martinique-style carving."

"Are you saying it's an antique?"

"I won't know for certain until I examine it closely."

"I have two steamer trunks filled with correspondence, bills, canceled checks and documents linked to this house. I haven't had the chance to go through everything except to pull out blueprints and floor plans."

"Would you mind if I take a look at them? Maybe I can find receipts to ascertain where a particular item was purchased."

"Are you sure that's what you want to do?"

Sonja turned to look at Taylor. "Yes, I'm sure. Some of these pieces could have been ordered from Europe or won at auction."

"I'll wait until you move into the hotel before I bring them over."

"I noticed we passed several motels during the drive here."

Taylor shook his head. "A few are not much better than flophouses. I much prefer one belonging to a chain. I'll set up an account for you once you check into an apartment suite where you will have the option of ordering room service or cooking for yourself. I'll give you a salary commensurate with your education and experience, and you can set your own hours. Once the property is secured, you will be given an electronic key card that will allow you access to come and go whenever you like."

"That sounds like an offer I can't refuse," she teased.

"I don't want you to refuse it. You're not going to become my employee, but a contract worker. Right now I don't have time to look for another architectural historian. It's going to be a lot easier finding painters, carpenters, and masons than someone with your expertise. I told you before that I don't yell or threaten, but I am no-nonsense when overseeing a project. I have a timeline as to when I want the exterior and interiors completed, and that's before my brothers leave their jobs to become involved with the business."

"What about Viola?"

Taylor's eyebrows lifted slightly. "I'm hoping she will eventually come around. But, if she doesn't then I'll contact culinary schools to recommend their best graduates."

"You really have everything figured out, don't you?"

"I have to. I owe it to my dad to fulfill his last wish to my mother."

Sonja noticed Taylor's voice had changed when he'd mentioned his father. There was no doubt the two had been very close. She wanted to tell him that she would do whatever she needed to help him fulfill his father's final request to his mother. "And I promise to assist you in making Bainbridge House a pretty girl again because she's been neglected far too long. She may have a little dinge, but it's nothing we can't get rid of."

He gave her skeptical look. "Are you saying Bainbridge House is a girl?"

"Of course she's a girl. Are you familiar with the French term *belle époque*? It means *beautiful epoch*."

"I've read about it. But that was a long time ago."

"It is a period in French history dating between 1880 and World War I, and because Bainbridge House is designed as a French château built in 1883 and falls within this architectural era, I think of her as a girl. But after she has been restored both inside and out she will once again become a stunning woman flaunting her beauty for those stopping long enough to marvel at her."

Taylor crossed his arms over his chest. "I don't want you to take offense because this may sound sexist. Once the exterior of the house is power washed it will appear pink, and traditionally that's a color usually attributed to girls."

"I'm not offended, Taylor. I happen to like the color, and if I ever have a girl I'll definitely would dress her in pink."

"You want children?"

Sonja went still, meeting his eyes. There was something in Taylor's query that annoyed her. Did he believe she was so career focused that she eschewed motherhood? Even before she'd agreed to marry Hugh Davies, they'd talked about starting a family after she'd earned her degree. She had become

Hugh's second wife, and although he was nearly twenty years her senior he claimed he was looking forward to becoming a father for the first time.

However, Sonja had known before they'd celebrated their second wedding anniversary that she had no intention of bringing a child into a hostile environment where his or her parents spent more time arguing than making love. Now, as a single woman, her plan was to have a career and children. Rather than give birth, she would foster and eventually adopt an older child or children.

"Yes. I plan to adopt."

"Good for you."

She was taken aback by his response. "Good for me?"

Taylor unfolded his arms and rested both hands on her shoulders. "Yes. There are too many children languishing in foster care that need a forever home."

With wide eyes, Sonja stared at Taylor like a deer caught in the bright beam of headlights. She couldn't help comparing him to her ex-husband. On a scale of one to ten Hugh came in at a low-two while Taylor was a ten. She'd found him to be open-minded and nonjudgmental. And, more importantly, he wasn't a sexist.

"You would rather adopt than have your own biological children?" she asked.

Sonja's question gave Taylor pause when he recalled his own upbringing. Elise was unable to have children, yet that hadn't stopped her from becoming a mother of five. "There's no reason why I couldn't have both, Sonja. A lot of couples have blended families with biological kids and adoptees of different races." He didn't tell her that he was talking about his own upbringing and family.

During a heart-to-heart discussion with Elise during one of their first Sunday meetings, she'd asked him if he ever intended to marry or if he wanted to father children. Taylor had been forthcoming when he told her yes to both. He wanted to fall in love, marry and start a family. And it didn't matter whether he fathered or adopted them. Elise had become emotional when he told her he knew he would become a good father because she and Conrad were the best role models for him to nurture the children he'd hoped to have.

"Do you realize you're an anomaly."

"Why would you say that?"

"I've met a lot of men that claim they prefer fathering their kids to adopting someone else's."

"I don't see a problem with that, Sonja. What I take exception to is their not taking care of their kids. Sometimes it is impossible for couples to live together, but that doesn't excuse a man from not having a relationship with his kids. Too often it becomes out of sight, out of mind."

Taylor didn't want to go on a rant and talk about men he'd known who were serial fathers and had felt the need to impregnate every woman with whom they'd had a relationship. And then there were those who were missing in action once a woman revealed she was carrying his child. It had had happened to his biological mother, who'd lived with her boyfriend, and once she discovered she was pregnant and told him, he disappeared. Aware of the circumstances surrounding his birth, Taylor had made it a practice to develop a relationship and always use protection whenever he slept with a woman.

He released Sonja's shoulders and took a step back. He'd enjoyed touching her, inhaling her sensual perfume and staring into the large dark eyes brimming with confidence. In fact, he'd enjoyed it much too much for him to remain emotionally disconnected.

"Now that we've established that Bainbridge House is a girl, I'd like to ask how you would decorate this bedroom to make it appear less crowded."

Sonja pressed her palms together. "The round table and chairs will have to go, and the armoire should be moved, facing the bed. Shelves in the armoire have to be removed if you want to install a flat screen. The console table, doubling as a desk, could be positioned under the window to take advantage of daylight. I suppose the bedside tables can stay where they are."

Taylor knew Sonja's suggestions would make the room less crowded and more inviting. He walked over and opened the door to a walk-in closet. "There's plenty of space for clothes and storage." He opened another door to the en suite bathroom. "Come, Sonja, and check out the bathroom."

Sonja stood next to him and snapped a picture of a sculptural sink on a ribbed column with brass fittings and a deep soaking claw-foot bathtub also with brass fittings. Then she took photos of the commode and bidet. "There's a fireplace!"

"The original plans included fireplaces in every bathroom suite on the first and second floors."

"Why only those two floors, Taylor?"

"Anyone that was a Bainbridge occupied the first two floors. The upper ones were reserved for guests."

Sonja laughed softly. "Were they trying to send a message that they didn't want their guests to wear out their welcome? Taking a bath in an unheated bathroom in the dead of a northeast winter had to be torture."

"I agree. Revised plans dated 1912 included running water and the installation of central heating." Taylor knew the house's electrical system had to be upgraded and Wi-Fi capability added, and the plumbing had to pass code before Bainbridge House could be licensed as a hotel.

"What are you going to do with the water closets?" Sonja asked.

"Convert them into spaces to keep linens and cleaning supplies for the housekeeping staff, and stockrooms to store personal products for the restrooms. The house has two elevators, but I won't know if they're operable until they have been inspected. We'll probably need two more elevators, but I'll have to confer with the architect to determine where they will be located."

"When you open Bainbridge House as a hotel and wedding venue, what will be the capacity?"

Taylor pinched the bridge of his nose as he attempted to recall the original floor plans for several rooms. "I believe the larger ballroom can hold three hundred and the smaller one somewhere around a hundred. I'm considering making modifications to the bedrooms. I'd like to remove walls to convert them into connecting suites. Right now, there are one hundred bedrooms and I doubt whether we'll be able to book that many rooms at any given time."

"How many connecting suites are you talking about?"

"Probably seventy-five. Bainbridge House has gone through a number of architectural and structurally modifications since 1889 and must undergo even more to make it viable as a business."

Sonja nodded. "Most of these mansions have servant quarters. Do the plans include one?"

"Yes. In fact, it is quite large, which may indicate the Bainbridges needed a full staff to keep the house operational. Once you go through the documents, you'll have to let me know how many were in their employ."

"I recall you saying something about cottages."

Taylor realized Sonja had remembered a lot of what he'd told her. Then he realized she must have an incredible memory if only to be able to identify thousands of years of relics and works of art. "The caretaker lives in one, which leaves five unoccupied."

"Does he live there with his family?"

"No. He's not married."

"What do you intend to do with the other five?" Sonja had asked yet another question.

Taylor's plans for the cottages included turning them into family residences. "Unlike the Bainbridges who occupied the first two floors in the main house, I plan to live in one of the cottages."

"What about the rest of your family?"

"We'll see when that time comes. The floor plans show one large bedroom and two smaller ones. There's also a kitchen, bathroom and an area for a living and dining room."

Taylor talking about the cottages had Sonja wondering what they had been used for when there was more than enough space in the main house to accommodate friends, guests and family members. If they weren't occupied by tenant farmers, then the only alternative could have been for guests who had insisted on complete privacy, or men of wealth and privilege who'd sequestered their mistresses on the property away from the prying eyes of their wives and her friends.

"Maybe the next time I come I'd like to see inside one," she told Taylor.

"I'll make certain they're cleaned and aired out.

Do you want to see a bedroom on the third or fourth floors?"

"No. I'd rather to go up to the turrets and look out over the property."

Taylor reached for her hand, and Sonja felt a slight shiver sweep up her arm. Whether Taylor was assisting her in or out of his SUV, resting his hand at the small of her back or touching her hand, it had become a struggle not to pretend she was a heroine in a romance novel and he the hero, and they would live happily ever after. Everything about him made her feel safe and protected. However, she had to remind herself she wasn't a character in a novel, but a real flesh-and-blood woman with deep-rooted trust issues when it came to men.

When she'd first walked into Professor Hugh Davies's classroom Sonja had been awestruck by the middle-aged man with the handsomeness of leading men in 1940s and 1950s movies. And when she'd glanced at the other female students, she realized their reaction was like hers: they were mesmerized. Professor Davies was the total package: tall, slender, perpetually tanned, and he'd been blessed with a velvety baritone voice.

He periodically conducted a slideshow quiz, and students were required to name a painting and painter or piece of sculpture. Because she'd been able to identify each slide every time, she'd believed he had taken a special interest in her whenever he'd asked her to stay after class to discuss her grades.

Her fellow students were unaware she'd grown up visiting European medieval cities with museums and churches displaying priceless artifacts.

Her passion with art also extended to photography and she owned coffee table books depicting black-and-white photographs of the celebration of Black culture and the struggle for freedom dating from 1840. Many of the photographs were now a part of the Smithsonian.

As a twenty-year-old art major at Boston College, Sonja hadn't realized she was in over her head with Hugh until it was too late. She hadn't told her mother she was involved with one of her professors until after they were married. There was complete silence on the other end of the call, and then the sound of a dial tone. Her mother had hung up on her. Telling Maria that Sonja had become the second wife of a man old enough to be her father had shocked and disappointed her mother. Her father's reaction was different. He'd wished her well. It was what he'd said next that proved prophetic. He said because she was an adult and responsible for her own actions, she had to be willing to accept all and any consequences of her marriage.

Although she thought of Taylor Williamson as the total package, there was no way she would allow her heart to rule her head. She'd married once, and that was something she did not want to repeat. Been there, done that. And she didn't need a man in order to have a baby because she had the option of adopting.

She glanced up at Taylor when he tightened his hold on her fingers as they climbed the winding staircase to the turrets. She noticed he wasn't breathing as heavily as she was from the exertion, which indicated he was in excellent physical condition.

"Do you work out?" she asked him.

He smiled at her. "Yes. There's a sports club for the residents in the development where I live."

"You told me you're moving into your mother's house. Is there space there where you can work out?"

"Yes. She has a condo in a gated development with a lot of on-site amenities. She's still staying at the house where I grew up. It's now on the market, and she's waiting for someone to buy it."

"Mortgage rate are low, so right now it's a buyer's market."

"True. But it's not your traditional three or four-bedroom home. It's a five-thousand-square-foot farmhouse built on four acres with an in-ground pool and tennis and basketball courts. With six bedrooms and seven baths, it would be perfect for a large or extended family."

Taylor's revelations that he'd lived on what Sonja thought of as an estate now confirmed her suspicions once she and Viola had become friends. Her friend had grown up privileged. Viola had revealed she and her brothers did not have to apply for student loans to subsidize their college tuitions and that her father had paid her rent on her West Village apartment until she'd secured permanent employment. Viola had also hinted her father had inherited a small fortune after the death of his parents, while Taylor had admitted his grandparents had set up a trust for his father, which he was able to gain access to at twenty-one. Even if Taylor hadn't grown up with the proverbial silver spoon in his mouth, it was purported he'd earned a great deal of money as a top male model.

Viola would talk incessantly about her brothers in glowing terms that made Sonja slightly unhappy she didn't share the same closeness with her brother because of their ten-year age gap. Viola said one of her brothers had married, but the union did not last a year, and another had recently proposed to his long-time girlfriend, while Taylor and another brother were still single. And she was adamant that Taylor did not want to be introduced to any of her gal friends, and the one time she ignored his warning he'd read her the riot act. Sonja was quick to tell Viola that she echoed his sentiments. She didn't want or need a man at this time in her life because her career took precedence over any relationship.

Sonja felt the muscles in her calves straining from climbing the staircase. "Will you continue to live with your mother once she sells her house?"

Taylor stopped at the top of the staircase and opened a narrow door. He walked in, glanced around and beckoned her to follow. "Yes. My mother is scheduled to take an around-the-world cruise. She says if she doesn't sell the house before August, then she'll close it up. I promised her I would check on it at least once a week."

"How long is her cruise?"

"Two hundred forty-five days."

"Well, damn," Sonja whispered under her breath.

Taylor chuckled, the sound rumbling in his chest. "That's what I said when she first told me about it. She claims she's making up for all the times she asked Dad to go on cruise with her, hoping he would change his mind about his parents' boating accident. Now that Dad's gone, she's convinced her best friend to be her cabinmate. They met as college roommates, and their friendship has spanned fifty-plus years."

"It's not often people remain friends that long. Either they move to another city or state, or their lives change once they marry and have a family. Most times, it's like life gets in the way of maintaining a friendship of that duration."

"Life got in the way and that's why you want nothing to do with men?"

Her jaw dropped and her mouth opened, but no words came out. She wondered if Viola had disclosed to Taylor the details of her failed marriage. Viola Williamson was as close to a friend that she could count or rely on, yet when she'd poured out her heart to the chef about how she'd allowed her husband to turn her life upside down, she hadn't told her to keep the conversation between just the two of them.

"Who said I want nothing to do with men?" Sonja

knew she sounded defensive, but at that point she didn't care.

"You did in so many words, Sonja. You're not married, don't have a boyfriend, and you plan to become a single mother. To me, that translates into you being content to live your life alone."

She glared at him. Taylor had no right to attempt to psychoanalyze her when he knew very little about who she was. "You make it sound as if I'm a man-hater," she spit out between clenched teeth as she struggled not to lose her temper.

Sonja walked over to the narrow window to give herself time to calm down. She didn't want to say something that would ruin her chance to become the architectural historian for the restoration project. She concentrated on the landscape unfolding before her eyes, taking deep breaths to slow down her respiration. She saw a pond with ducks and swans. Her gaze shifted, and she spied the roof of one of the cottages. She went completely still when she felt the heat from Taylor's body seep through her jacket and into her when he pressed his chest against her back.

"I didn't say you were a man-hater, Sonja," he whispered in her ear. "And I'm not accusing you of being lonely. Being alone and lonely are not the same."

Sonja knew she didn't have to explain herself to Taylor, especially if he was to become her employer. And it wasn't because she was his sister's friend. It was her education and experience in the field of art history that made him want her to become a part of his restoration team.

She turned to face him. "What are you saying, Taylor, if not that?"

He stared down her at the same time the beginnings of a smile tilted the corners of his strong mouth. "I think you are an incredibly talented woman that any man with half a brain would respect."

Sonja felt hot tears pricking the back of her eyelids, but she refused to cry and embarrass herself. Hugh had driven her to tears so many times that he would provoke her just to see her cry. She was damned and determined not to let Taylor see her that way.

"I had a man tell me almost those exact words and, unfortunately, I fell hard, hook, line and sinker, into his trap. I gave him four years of my life, and then I knew I had to get out before I allowed him to destroy me. It took another two years to end the legal entanglement because he refused to let me go. That's when I swore I would never become involved with another controlling man as long as I was in my right mind."

"You are lucky because you were able to get on with your life. I know you don't want to hear it, but not all men are like your ex-husband."

Sonja closed her eyes for a few seconds. "It's been difficult for me, but that's something I've been trying to convince myself."

"I'm not saying I'll try to convince you one way or the other, but I'm available if you need a friend."

She managed a brittle smile. "You want to be my friend *and* my boss?"

One of Taylor's eyebrows lifted. "Boss aside, I'll always make myself available to you if you need to talk about something."

Sonja chided herself for misinterpreting his motives. Maybe it was because she was his sister's friend that he didn't want any romantic entanglement. Besides, he'd warned Viola about attempting to set him up with her friends, and for Sonja she thought of it as a win-win. Not only would she add the restoration project to her résumé, she would also interact with a man with whom she could have a no-pressure ongoing friendship.

She extended her right hand. "All right. Friends."

Taylor took her hand and dropped a kiss on her fingers. "Friends." He released her hand. "Now, friend, it's time we head down to the cellar so you can see what's waiting for you."

Chapter Five

Sonja clapped a hand over her mouth when she saw crates filled with china, paintings, crystal pieces, monogrammed silverware, a collection of snuff boxes, framed prints, porcelain figurines, vases and military swords and paraphernalia, and worn leather-bound books she suspected were first editions.

She found shelves lined with dusty wine bottles, Bainbridge Cellars labels indicating the year the grapes were harvested. The entire cellar contained a treasure trove of items that would take months, possibly a year, to go through.

"What do you think?"

She turned to find Taylor standing several feet away, arms crossed over his chest. "I feel like a kid walking into FAO Schwarz during the Christmas holiday season. I don't know where to begin."

"I told you it was overwhelming."

She sighed. "Yes, you did. I'm going tackle one crate at a time, but I can't work down here." The space was dimly illuminated with several overhead naked bulbs.

"Don't worry, Sonja. I'll set aside a room you can use as an office. And once you're set up, I'll bring the steamer trunks here instead of leaving them at your hotel. You'll have enough to do here, that once you get back to your hotel you shouldn't have to look at anything that remotely resembles work."

"Thank you." She paused. "I'm sure there's a library in the house, and that would be perfect place to set up my office."

Taylor lowered his arms. "Let's go upstairs and see."

They found the library on the east wing of the château. Sonja stared at the walls. "You'll have to hire faux bois specialists to restore the wall, and the plaster moldings in here and in the ballrooms," she told Taylor.

"After I take care of securing and cleaning the house, I'll need you to come back and go through the entire house and recommend the craftspeople needed to restore everything to its original state."

"That's not a problem. The interiors have held up well after not being occupied for sixty years. I've been inside homes that were practically falling around the owner's head because of neglect. Bainbridge House has what I call good bones."

"We'll find out once I inspect the foundation."

"When are you going to do that?" she asked.

"One day this week. A moving company is scheduled to take the contents of my apartment to a storage unit sometime next week. Once that's done I can move into my mother's condo. Living in Jersey…" His words trailed off. "Is that your stomach making those noises?"

Sonja bit her lip as she averted her gaze. "Yes. All I had was coffee, and it's probably reminding me that I need to eat."

"Why didn't you say something earlier? We could've stopped to eat before coming here." Reaching into the pocket of his jeans he removed his cell phone and tapped the screen. "I just sent Dom a message that we're leaving, and he should close the windows and the gate."

Sonja was relieved to leave the cavernous unheated house and feel the warmth of the sun on her face. She'd hoped by the time the office was set up for her to begin working she wouldn't have to wear a coat.

"Where are we going to eat?" she asked Taylor as she secured her seat belt.

"There's a restaurant in Yonkers I sometimes frequent. The food and service are excellent."

She shared a smile with him. "All right. Let's go."

Taylor winked at her. "Yes, ma'am."

* * *

"How's your omelet?"

Sonja's fork stopped in midair as she smiled across the table at Taylor. They'd arrived at the restaurant as brunch diners were leaving and were able to get a table in the enclosed patio with views of the Hudson River. "It's delicious." She'd ordered the farmer's omelet with a medley of finely diced peppers, onions, mushrooms, bacon, ham and sausage. "How did you find this place?" Taylor had had to drive down several narrow one-way streets before he was able to find parking.

"I told you my college buddies used to search out restaurants to visit, and one day we missed the turnoff for City Island. We decided to keep heading north and ended up here."

"I thought you said you took the subway uptown and to other boroughs."

Taylor gave her a direct stare. "Do you remember everything I say?"

"Just about," she admitted.

"Which means you could catch me in a lie."

"Do you lie?" she asked, deadpan.

"Hardly ever," Taylor countered. "I learned a long time ago that if you tell a lie, then you have to tell another to correct that one, and after a while you're busted."

Sonja popped a piece of fluffy egg into her mouth, chewed and then swallowed it. "Back to my question about how you ended up in Yonkers. Whose car did you use?"

"It was my rental."

"Renting a car under the age of twenty-five is pricey."

"Not for me, Sonja, because I'd just turned twenty-five."

"How did you get into modeling?"

"I sort of fell into it."

Propping her elbow on the table, she cupped her chin in the heel of her hand. "Tell me how you fell into it."

There had been a time in his life when he'd forgotten his career goals. He'd known at ten when his parents gave him a Christmas gift of Lego that he'd fancied himself a builder. Using the interlocking pieces, he spent hours creating entire cities with imaginary office buildings, hospitals, restaurants and even malls. Instead of his obsession waning as he grew older, it intensified. Whenever he went into Manhattan with his father he'd found himself transfixed with the towering buildings and wondering how they were able to stand without falling.

"Earth to Taylor."

He smiled. "I'm sorry about zoning out on you."

"Are you or aren't you going to tell me how you became a model?"

Now he knew why Sonja and Viola were friends. They were like dogs with bones when seeking information. "I'd just begun my sophomore year at NYU when a student asked if she could take some photos of me for a photography project because she said I had an interesting face. I told her I would think about it, but then she told me not to think too long because she had to complete her project and submit it in a couple of days. I said okay and she gave me a form to fill out with my name, address and phone number. There was also a section certifying that she owned the photographs.

"I met her the next day in one of the classrooms set up as art studios, and after about twenty minutes she was finished."

"Did you have to take off your clothes?"

Taylor wagged a finger. "Get your mind out of the gutter, Ms. Rios-Martin. I wasn't auditioning for a porno flick."

She narrowed her eyes. "But you did take off a few garments."

Taylor wondered if he was that transparent or she that perceptive. "She did ask me to remove my shirt and shoes."

"Even if she'd asked you to take off all of your clothes, as an artist she would've viewed your nude body as art."

"I'm not a prude, but I wouldn't have complied in case she wasn't going to use the photos for her school project."

"Did you know her?"

"Not personally, but I would see her around campus and always with a camera. I ran into her a month later, and she told me that her professor gave her an A. Her prof said I might do well if she sent the photos to a modeling agency. I told her to do it just to humor her. I'd returned to Jersey for the winter break when I got a call from a woman asking if she could rep me because a modeling agency was interested in booking me.

"I'd forgotten about the pictures until she mentioned the photographer's name. I was curious, so I agreed to meet her at a midtown restaurant. I listened to her spiel and told her I had to talk it over with my parents. Mom and Dad really didn't want me to drop out, but I promised then I would do it for two years, and then go back to school. Two years turned into five and even though I'd earned a lot of money I knew it wasn't what I wanted to do long term."

"So, you just walked away." Sonja's question was a statement.

"Yes. And I've never regretted it."

"How did you manage to remain an enigma when your face was so recognizable?"

Other women had questioned him about his career as a model and most times he was able to gloss over it without going into detail about a time in his life when he'd lost focus on his goal to become an engineer. However, Taylor felt differently when it came to Sonja. Not only was she his sister's friend, but they would also work together and he wanted her to trust him.

"I had a clause in my contract prohibiting the agency from disclosing anything about my personal life. Professionally I'd become T.E. Wills, while in private I could be Taylor Edward Williamson."

"What I don't understand, Taylor, is once you become a public figure it's virtually impossible for you to claim you want your privacy. Fame isn't arbitrary or negotiable."

"I know that. I insisted on privacy to protect my family more than myself. I knew how my life would change the instant my image appeared in a commercial or on the page of a slick magazine, but no one in my family wanted their lives disrupted or dissected because I'd chosen a career where I was earning money using my face and body."

"I was in my nail salon when I picked up *People*'s Most Beautiful issue—in which you were included."

Taylor rolled his eyes upward. "Please don't remind me of that. That was a couple of weeks before I was scheduled to retire, but my agent pleaded with me to go to the shoot. I really did it as a favor to her."

Sonja wanted to tell Taylor that his favor had extended to millions of women because he was the epitome of elegance as he leaned against a low-slung sports car in formal dress with a mischievous smile parting his lips. His expression was hypnotic and inviting.

"Going out on top means you'll never be labeled a has-been."

Throwing back his head, Taylor laughed. "A has-been at twenty-four is really a stretch."

"Don't laugh, Taylor. Think of all the child actors that weren't able to transition to adult roles."

He sobered. "You're right."

"What's going to happen when you open Bainbridge House as a hotel, and it's covered by the press? Then the whole world will know that Taylor Williamson is the legendary T.E. Wills."

"I doubt…" His words trailed off when Sonja's cell phone rang. "Aren't you going to answer that?"

Sonja recognized Viola's ringtone. Reaching into her cross-body, she tapped the screen. "Hello."

"Hey, girl. I'm calling to find out how it went with my brother last night."

"Can I call you later?"

"Are you with him now?"

"Yes."

"Don't forget to call me."

"I won't. Later." Sonja ended the call, set the phone on the table next to her plate and picked up her napkin, touching it to the corners of her mouth. "I don't think I can eat any more." The three-egg omelet was very filling.

Taylor raised his hand to signal for their waitress. "Do you want dessert to take home?"

"No, thank you. My aunt is watching my uncle's sugar intake, and I would be sabotaging him if I brought dessert home."

"Speaking of home, it's time we headed out, and beat the traffic."

* * *

"My building is at the end of the block," Sonja told Taylor as slowed along the tree-lined street and maneuvered into an empty space. She unbuckled her belt. "Thank you for everything."

Taylor also removed his belt. "I'll walk you in."

Sonja rested a hand on his arm. "It's okay. My building is pretty safe."

He met her eyes. "Are you sure?"

"Yes, Taylor." Leaning to her left, she kissed his cheek. "Later."

She knew she'd shocked him with the gesture, and got out unassisted and walked toward her building. After entering the vestibule, she unlocked the inner door and made her way to the elevator. She'd just gotten in the car when her phone's text tone vibrated. Sonja pushed the button for the tenth floor and then tapped the icon for messages.

Taylor had sent her a contract offering the average salary for museum director or curator. It was more than double what she earned working at the gallery. She hadn't broached the topic of salary with him because she had wanted him to make the first overture. Well, he had, and now she would be able to save enough to purchase a condo sooner rather than later.

Sonja exited the car when it stopped at her floor. Her step was light when she strolled down the hallway to the apartment. She unlocked the door, closed it and left the camera case on a chair in the entryway. She tossed her keys in a large candy dish and then sat on the chair to remove her boots, leaving them on the mat inside the door.

The flat screen was off in the living room, indicating she was alone in the apartment. Her uncle turned on the television as soon as he got up and didn't turn it off until he retired for bed. She went into her bedroom, changed out of her street clothes and into a pair of cotton drawstring pants and oversized tee. Settling into a cushioned rocker, Sonja retrieved her cell phone and sent him a grinning face emoji, and then tapped Viola's number.

"Tell me everything and don't you dare leave anything out."

"What happened to 'hello, Sonja'?"

"Hello, Sonja. Now please tell me everything."

"I've decided to work with Taylor on the restoration project."

"I knew that would happen. But, what about you and Taylor?"

"What about us, Vi?"

"Do you like him?"

"What's not to like? I must admit I was shocked to discover he is T.E. Wills."

There was a pause before Viola said, "I couldn't tell you because he really values his privacy. I know that sounds crazy when he is so recognizable. My family has more than its share of secrets. I never told any man I dated that my dad came from wealthy family, because I didn't want to be viewed as a dollar sign. You know a lot more about me than a lot of people because I trust you, Sonja."

"Yeah, right," she drawled. "You trusted me so much that you didn't tell me your gorgeous brother was a top male model."

Viola's sultry laugh came through the earpiece. "Sorry about that."

Sonja pushed out her lips even though Viola couldn't see her. "I got to see the château today."

"What do you think of it? It reminds me of Disney's Magic Kingdom."

"It's beautiful."

"You would say that because I know how much you love old buildings and castles."

"You don't like it, Vi?"

"It's not that I don't like it. What I am is ambivalent. Taylor wants me to take over the kitchen once the hotel is up and running, but I'm still not certain that's what I want to do."

"Why not? Is it that you don't believe you have enough experience to be the executive chef?"

"Maybe not now, but I'm certain I will be in a couple of years."

"Don't play yourself, Viola. You went to one of the top culinary schools in the country and graduated at the top of your class. And you're talented enough to have secured a position at a Michelin-starred restaurant. Women executive chefs are still as scarce as hen's teeth, while you're dragging your feet about whether you want to become involved in your family's business."

"I don't know if I have the personality to supervise a commercial kitchen. Besides, I need more experience. Right now, I'm waiting to be promoted from a line cook to sous-chef."

"Stop making excuses, Viola."

"I'm not making excuses, Sonja. Running a kitchen is a daunting task and at this time in my life I don't feel confident enough to become an executive chef."

"Do you realize how many times you've complained about your tyrannical boss who gets his jollies off browbeating his staff?"

A beat passed. "I suppose too many times," Viola admitted. "But I've learned to tune him out."

"You shouldn't have to tune him out, Vi, when you're not obligated to stay on once Bainbridge House opens for business. I'm looking forward to the grand opening when you and your brothers gather in front of the mansion for a ribbon-cutting ceremony—you in your chef's whites with Bainbridge House, Viola Williamson, Executive Chef embroidered on your coat."

"Why do you make it sound so over-the-top?"

Sonja smiled. "Because it would be. Food critics will be lining up to eat at Bainbridge House, and then writing about the food and service. And I'm willing to bet there will be articles in cooking magazines about you being an up-and-coming chef to watch."

Viola laughed. "Maybe I should hire you as my publicist."

"You don't need a publicist, Vi. Your dishes will speak for themselves."

"I'm not going to promise anything, but I'll tell you what I told Taylor. I'll think about it."

"Don't think too long, Vi. Time will go by faster than you think." Sonja wanted to tell her friend she'd short-circuited her own career when she opted to marry rather than complete her education. And while she hadn't been able to make up for the lost years Sonja had made herself a promise to maintain her emotional wellbeing at the same time making her career a priority.

"I know. I can't believe I'm having second thoughts even though I've always wanted to run my own kitchen. My real quandary is giving up my apartment and moving back to New Jersey. You know how much I love living in the Village."

Sonja did not want to debate with Viola that moving across the river paled in comparison to the possibility of making a name for herself in a male-dominated field. "I know, Vi, but you have to think of yourself as a role model for not only women, but particularly women of color who want a career in culinary arts."

"I've never thought of myself as a role model, but you always know what to say to bring me back to reality."

"I learned it from you, my friend. When we first

met, I was still healing emotionally. You listened to me go on and on about my ex and what he'd done to me. Then you told me that I had to stop blaming myself for someone else's negative behavior."

"I had a similar experience with a guy I'd believed was the love of my life. When I found out he was cheating on me I told him it was over. He pleaded and begged, said that it would never happen again. I forgave him over and over until I realized he would always be a serial cheater. The only way I could get over him was to go into therapy. It took more than six months for me to completely exorcise him not only from my life but also my head."

Sonja was slightly taken aback with her friend's revelation. Viola rarely talked about her past relationships. She'd mentioned occasionally dating yet never admitted to having had a serious relationship. "Fortunately, I didn't have to lay on a therapist's couch because I had you to give it to me straight, no chaser."

"I know there are times when I'm a little too candid for my own good, and that's when Taylor has accused me of not having a filter."

"I've concluded it is better to speak up rather than remain silent." Sonja knew she wasn't the same woman who'd fallen under the spell of a much older man and married him. She didn't hate men. She was just wary of their motives. However, it would be different with Taylor. They would be friends.

She chatted with Viola for few more minutes and then ended the call.

Last summer Taylor's sister had hosted a Sunday brunch buffet at her apartment and Sonja had been amazed with what she'd prepared. The gathering was small—less than a dozen people—and included Viola's waitstaff coworkers, her roommate's colleagues and her neighbors. One of her neighbors that had taken an interest in Sonja, and everywhere she turned he was only a few feet away. Then he'd asked if they could go somewhere later that evening for drinks. She had turned him down politely with the excuse that someone was coming to pick her up at six. Of course, he didn't believe her and offered to walk her down to the street. She was hard-pressed not to laugh at his crestfallen expression when she got into the car with Jaime. Her cousin had proved invaluable when it came to discouraging men attempting to come onto her.

She retrieved her camera, booted up her laptop and downloaded the photos she'd taken at Bainbridge House. Sonja had described the mansion as having a little dinge, which did not in any way diminish the graceful beauty of the architecture.

She had just enlarged the photos of moldings in the library and the smaller ballroom when her phone rang. Glancing at the screen she saw Taylor's name. She tapped the speaker feature. "I hope you're driving hands free."

His deep laugh caressed her ear. "I'm not driving. I'm home."

"How did you get there so quickly?"

"Stamford is only thirty miles from Inwood."

"That's all?"

"That's it. Should I interpret your emoji to mean that you've accepted my salary offer?"

Sonja bit on her lip to keep from laughing. "Yes."

"Good. Send me your email address, and I'll have Patrick send you a list of documents he'll need for your personnel file. I know he'll want a résumé and unofficial copies of your college transcripts. He'd wanted to ask for letters of recommendation, but I told him I'd vouch for you. He's setting up payroll for direct deposit so he will need your banking information. I'm projecting your start day will be the first week in May. Meanwhile, I'll search for hotels in the area and instruct Patrick to set up a corporate account for you. It will be the same with the leased car. I'll arrange for it to be delivered to you the day you check into the hotel. You're going to need a credit card for anything that's business related. Just make certain to save the receipts because my brother is—excuse the expression—a tight-ass CPA who will go ballistic if he can't account for every penny."

"Tight-ass or scrooge?"

"Both. I'm willing to go along with his edicts because Patrick is a genius when it comes to accounting and taxation."

* * *

"Will I get to meet him?" Sonja asked.

"I doubt it. Right now, he's living in Napa with his fiancée. She comes from a family of winemakers. A few years back Patrick worked for her uncle, who'd begun a startup vineyard on Long Island's North Shore. Next year will be the first time from the initial planting that they will get their first harvest. He told me the first vintage probably won't be bottled for another two years after that."

Sonja recalled dozens of dusty and cobweb-covered wine bottles in the château's cellar. "Does he plan to become the vintner for Bainbridge Cellars?"

Taylor's sigh reverberated through the speaker. "I'm hoping he will. But, if he doesn't, then I'm going to bring in a wine taster to judge the quality of the wine in the cellar. If he gives it a thumbs-up, then I'm willing to hire a vintner and workers to restore the vineyard and put in new plantings."

"I just had an idea, Taylor."

"Talk to me, sweetheart."

Sonja went completely still, wondering if Taylor had meant to call her 'sweetheart,' or if the endearment had slipped out unconsciously. "You'd talked about the gardens and orchard, but have you given any thought to putting in a farm?"

"What type of farm?"

"A vegetable farm. After all, New Jersey *is* touted as the Garden State."

"That it is, but who's going to maintain the farm?"

"Really, Taylor? You hire someone. You'll save a lot of money if you grow your own produce in greenhouses year-round and offer farm-to-table dining."

A beat passed. "Do you have any other suggestions?"

"I have a few more."

"Do you want to tell me about them?"

Sonja smiled when she registered laughter in Taylor's query. "I'll wait until I see you again."

"I'm always open to your suggestions as long as they are within the realm of possibility."

"Like raising chickens, ducks and sheep?"

"That's enough, Sonja. I have no intention of operating Old MacDonald's farm."

"Why not? You'll have stables for horses, so why not house the chickens, ducks and sheep in the barn? There's nothing better than fresh chicken and duck eggs."

"Where is all of this coming from?"

His accusatory tone was beginning to annoy Sonja. "Forget it, Taylor."

"No, Sonja, I'm not going to forget it."

"We don't have to talk about it now. The next time we get together I'll have put everything on paper."

"Okay."

"After I hang up I'll text you my email."

"Okay," Taylor repeated.

"I'll talk to you later." Sonja ended the call. If Taylor had been willing to listen without prejudice,

Sonja would have explained she'd toured the Loire Valley and had stopped to eat at a château offering farm-to-table meals. The owners raised their own chickens and ducks, and the difference between store-bought refrigerated eggs and ones gathered daily were remarkable. It was the same with the freshly picked vegetables and free-range poultry.

As promised, Sonja would write down her ideas, suggestions and recommendations, and present them to Taylor. It wouldn't bother her if he rejected them— just the fact that he would take the time to listen was enough. She texted Taylor her email address and then returned her attention to the photos she'd taken at Bainbridge House.

A knock on her bedroom door got her attention. She smiled. Her aunt had come home. "Hi, Titi Yolie." Sonja shifted on the bench seat in front of the table where she'd set her laptop and printer. "Come and see the pictures I took of the mansion."

Yolanda walked in, sat beside Sonja and slowly shook her head. "That's what I call wretched excess. I'll never understand why rich folks in this country felt the need to build these monstrosities."

"During the Gilded Age, America's nouveau riche flaunted their wealth to emulate European royalty," Sonja explained. "They had everything but the titles, while Europe's landed gentry needed money to run their estates and were willing to trade their titles for cash. It became a win-win when young American heiresses married English nobility to become a princess, duchess, viscountess or a marchioness. Winston Churchill's mother was an American socialite, Consuelo Vanderbilt married the Duke of Marlborough, and Princess Diana's American great-grandmother had been a baroness."

"That's so tacky. Selling yourself for a title."

"Word," Sonja said in agreement. "American heiresses that married into the British aristocracy were referred to as 'Dollar Princesses.' Marrying an aristocrat was seen as a way for them to raise their social status."

"That's crazy, Sonja. If they are millionairesses, shouldn't that be status enough?"

"Not for them. They were the daughters of self-made men who didn't have the social standing of longtime members of high society."

"Are you saying they were shunned?" Yolanda asked.

"Yes, because they were new and not old money, and they'd believed a title would enhance their position among America's social elite. Unfortunately for some of these titled princesses they did not have a happily-ever-after. Princess Diana's great-grandmother divorced her husband, while Consuelo Vanderbilt also divorced her husband."

Yolanda snorted delicately. "What did they expect when they sold themselves just to be accepted by those that looked down on them because they didn't have the proper pedigree."

"You are preaching to the choir, Auntie."

"Now that you've seen the mansion, are you going to accept the commission to help restore it?"

"Yes." Sonja knew she'd shocked her aunt when she revealed she would have to live in New Jersey. "I don't want to drive ninety minutes to work, put in six or seven hours, and then sit in a car for another ninety-plus minutes in rush hour traffic, to turn around and do it again the next day."

"When are you leaving?"

Sonja draped an arm around her aunt's shoulders. "Not until early May."

"I suppose that means you'll be leaving the gallery."

"Yes. I will let them know that I'll stay until that time." Sonja knew that once she become a part of the restoration team, her life and her future would not be the same. She was looking forward to her involvement in the restoration.

"What do you know about the family that built this mansion?"

"Not much," Sonja admitted truthfully. She would set aside as much time as necessary to research the Bainbridges and hopefully discover Taylor's father's connection to the wealthy family that had erected an exact replica of a French château in northern New Jersey.

Chapter Six

Taylor took one last look around the apartment and then left the keys, as instructed by the building manager, on the kitchen countertop. The movers had come earlier that morning and transported the boxes to their van to take them to a storage unit near his mother's condo. Meanwhile, he'd packed and stored his clothes, personal items and the steamer trunks in the cargo area of the SUV. He'd called Elise to let her know he planned to stop and see her in Belleville before they drove up to Sparta.

His week had begun with him going to Bainbridge House because the security company was scheduled to wire the house and install cameras around the property. Even with a team of eight technicians it had taken nearly a week to set up everything. The caretaker had admitted he felt more secure now that the property was electronically monitored.

Taylor found Elise sitting on the porch knitting, the familiar rhythmic clicking of the needles reminding him of a time when his mother spent her spare time knitting sweaters, gloves, scarfs and hats for his sister and brothers. If she wasn't knitting, she could be found reading. Although a woman came in three days a week to clean and do laundry, Elise had insisted on preparing meals for her family.

Walking up the porch steps, Taylor leaned over and pressed his lips to his mother's graying strawberry-blond hair. "Hello, beautiful."

A flush suffused Elise's face following his compliment. When the social worker had brought him to the home of Elise Williamson, Taylor had believed she was a princess. He'd been told the tall, slender woman with a pale complexion, wavy reddish hair and sapphire-blue eyes was to become his new mother. She had insisted he call her Mom even though, at six, he knew she couldn't be his mother because his cousins looked like his aunt, and all of the kids in his class looked like their mothers. His greatest fear was going to school and having this woman come and identify herself as his mother and having his classmates laugh or call him a liar. It was only when he realized he didn't have to leave the house to attend classes, and that his foster mother had planned to homeschool him, that Taylor's fears vanished and he was able to call her Mom.

"You should be sweet-talking a young woman around your age instead of your seventy-two-year-old momma."

"I don't have time to sweet-talk anyone, Mom."

She gave him a long, penetrating stare as he folded his body down on a rocker facing hers. "I hope you don't get so caught up in restoring your father's property that you forget to relax."

Stretching out long legs, Taylor crossed his booted feet at the ankles. "I'd wanted to ask you about Dad's property."

Elise's hands stilled. "What do you want to know?"

"When did Dad know he'd inherited Bainbridge House?" He had learned not to ask Conrad about his family because the older man would give him a look that told him that he was prying. It was Elise who had occasionally revealed a few incidents in her husband's life that he'd loathed talking about.

"It was after his aunt died. He'd talked about owning land in the northern part of the state, but whenever I asked him what he intended to do with it he claimed he didn't know. A couple of months after he sold his company he took me to see it. I was so shocked that I was at a loss for words. Before that, he'd had the property appraised with the intention of selling it, and because he didn't say anything I'd assumed he'd sold it."

"Did he ever live at Bainbridge House?"

"Yes. He said he lived there before his parents' boating accident. He said he loved riding the horses. And when the ewes had lambs, he would give them all names. He said the caretaker didn't have to cut grass in the area where the sheep grazed because they were four-footed lawn mowers."

Taylor bit back a smile. Sonja had talked about chickens, ducks and sheep. "Why didn't you tell us about this before Easter Sunday?"

Leaning to her right, Elise put her knitting into a quilted bag beside her chair on the floor. "Conrad added a codicil to his will, and it wasn't until the reading of the will that was I made aware that he'd left the estate to me and his children. Meanwhile, I wanted to wait until the entire family was together to give everyone the news."

Taylor pressed his head against the back of the rocker and stared at the glass-topped wicker table and matching chairs in a corner of the wraparound porch. "If you were shocked when you first saw Bainbridge House, I know I speak for the others when I say we were also stunned by it."

"I'm glad you decided to take the lead when you said you would supervise the restoration, because if you hadn't, then I don't think Joaquin and Tariq would've agreed to join you."

"You underestimate them, Mom. I believe given the option of working for someone or one's self, most would choose the latter."

"Maybe for you, Tariq and Joaquin, but not Viola and Patrick."

"Patrick is involved, Mom. Don't forget he's overseeing the project's fiscal component. And I'd rather have him signing checks than a stranger."

Minute lines fanned out around Elise's eyes when she smiled. "You're right about that. Patrick is more nitpicky than Conrad ever was when it comes to money."

Taylor had to agree with his mother. His father had a sixth sense when it came to investing his clients' money, but it was Patrick's gift of total recall that proved invaluable to the company's ongoing profitability.

"That's four out of five, Taylor. I need you to convince Viola to join the rest of the family."

"You know if you tell Viola to go left, then she'll go right. Although she's always talked about running her own kitchen, I feel she'll come around even before we open as a hotel and wedding venue."

"I hope you're right."

Taylor wanted to tell his mother he knew he was right. Within days of Viola graduating culinary school, her future plans included opening her own restaurant. Every once in a while she would bring up the topic, and whenever Conrad offered to give her the start-up capital, her comeback was always she needed to be more experienced.

There was a swollen silence before Taylor asked his mother a question that had been nagging at him for months. "Are you selling this house and taking an extended cruise so you won't be reminded of Dad?"

Elise closed her eyes, and when she opened them they were shimmering with unshed tears. "It doesn't matter where I go because I'll never be able to forget Conrad. I knew he was special the first time he bumped into me at Princeton and spilled coffee on the front of my sweater. I yelled at him for not looking where he was going. He calmly told me he was sorry and would buy me another sweater. I told him I didn't want another sweater, and there was no way I could go to class with brown stains on my white sweater and smelling like coffee."

"Did you skip class?"

"No. Conrad took off his sweater and gave it to me. He stood there in just an undershirt. He told me to take off my sweater and he would have it cleaned. I told him there was no way I was going strip in front of him. The impasse ended when I walked behind a tree and exchanged my sweater for his, because all I had on was a bra. I gave him my off-campus address, and a week later he showed up with a box from Bloomingdale's with a cashmere twinset in a beautiful shade of cobalt blue. When I told him I couldn't accept something that expensive because I didn't know him, he claimed if I allowed him to take me out to dinner, then we could get to know each other."

Taylor laughed softly. "It looks as if Dad knew what to do and say to get his woman."

Elise's laughter joined his. "That he did. We set up

a date for dinner, and when he picked me up in his dinged-up two-seater sports car I was wearing the twinset with a strand of my grandmother's pearls. To say I was impressed is an understatement. Not only was I, a sophomore, going out with a senior, but I was totally unaware that he'd been born into wealth."

"When did you find that out?"

"The day he proposed marriage. By that time, I was so much in love with him that I couldn't say no even if I'd felt I was too young to marry. My father, who was a judge, married us, and we had a small reception on the patio with relatives and a few of my sorority sisters in attendance. He'd invited his aunt, but she'd declined because she had come down with pneumonia and her doctor had recommended she remain at home. We delayed going on a honeymoon until she recovered, but unfortunately she never did. Conrad honored her wishes to have her cremated, and four months after our wedding we were finally able to take our delayed honeymoon to Hawaii. We were living with my parents because we were waiting for this house to be renovated. Conrad had bought it below market value because it been abandoned for years.

"Meanwhile, I'd gone back to school to get a graduate degree in education. I'd just begun teaching when I discovered I was pregnant. I knew something was wrong because I kept cramping. I left school early and called my doctor to let him know I was coming in. I'd just walked in when I began hemorrhaging. I don't remember anything after that, but hours later when I woke up in the hospital was told that I'd lost my baby, and because they couldn't stop the bleeding I'd undergone a hysterectomy."

Elise sucked in a breath, holding it until she finally let it out. "I went into a depression because I realized I would never give Conrad children. When I told him this, he said we could always adopt. It was when I spoke to my former college roommate who'd become a social worker that she convinced me to become a foster parent, because the adoption process was a lengthy one." She smiled. "That's when I got you."

Taylor's smile matched Elise's. "You got me, and then you couldn't stop until you filled every bedroom in this house."

"That's because you were the sweetest little boy any mother could wish for. Then I rolled the dice and requested another foster child. I'm not going to say it was easy raising children who had been neglected and had experienced a myriad of traumas, but I was willing to accept the challenge. And once I decided to homeschool you and saw you thrive, I knew that's what I wanted for the others. My mother accused me of setting up a safety net for my children where they wouldn't be able to survive outside the bubble I'd created."

Taylor hadn't had much interaction with Elise's parents, who'd relocated to Florida to take advantage of the warmer climate. "Thankfully, they did live long enough to see us survive."

"You're right. My mother finally had to admit that Conrad and I had done a good job raising their grandchildren."

Taylor would readily admit to anyone that he'd had the best upbringing any child could wish for. Although Conrad was a workaholic, putting in long hours at his office Monday through Friday, on the weekends he devoted himself totally to his wife and children. Once the family increased, he'd arranged for an in-ground pool and basketball and tennis courts. On Saturdays or Sundays, he could be seen shooting hoops with his sons and daughter or swimming laps with Viola.

"And I'm certain once Patrick marries and has children he will also become a good father."

Elise's mouth twisted into a sneer. "I shouldn't say this, but I really don't like my future daughter-in-law."

Taylor angled his head. "Why would you say that?"

"She's a bit too pushy and immature for my tastes. When Patrick doesn't do what she wants, she tends to pout like a little child."

Taylor wanted to tell Elise he agreed with her but didn't think it was his place to comment on his brother's choice as a potential wife. "It's apparent that it doesn't bother him."

"Well, I still don't like her," Elise mumbled under her breath.

He sat straight, wondering if his mother would approve of the woman he would choose as a wife. "I'm ready to move into your condo."

Elise stood, Taylor pushing off the rocker and rising with her. "I just have to get my keys."

Sonja had drawn up a list of things she had to do before she relocated to New Jersey. She'd handed in her resignation, giving the gallery owners two weeks' notice. In the interim she'd gone through her closet to select garments for spring and summer, and then went online to purchase a number of tees and khakis that she'd planned to make her work ensemble, along with boots and running shoes.

She and Taylor communicated with each other electronically, either texting or emailing her with updates and emojis. He sent her a thumbs-up after it'd taken the security company a week to set up their system, and a thumbs-down after the maintenance company used more than a dozen workers over the span of a month to clean the entire house from the turrets to the cellar.

When she wasn't working at the gallery, Sonja went online to research Bainbridge House and had gleaned more about the house than the family for which it had been named. However, she did discover an article written about Charles Garland Bainbridge that recorded he'd been prevented from building his summer cottage in Newport, Rhode Island, like millionaire owners of The Breakers, Marble House and Chateau-sur-Mer because there were rumors that his wife may have been a mulatto. Sonja was anxious to go through the contents of the trunks to uncover what secrets the Bainbridge family wanted to hide or deny.

Bainbridge House had survived while Newport's summer retreats of wealthy Gilded Age industrialists hadn't after World War II. The Victorian-era mansions had become impractical and out of style. Many were converted into schools or condos, and others were neglected, razed or abandoned until the Preservation Society of Newport County began buying up Gilded Age mansions and opening them to the public as museums.

She'd just finished packing a Pullman when her cell phone rang. Smiling, she picked it up. "What's up, boss?"

Sonja did not realize how much she'd missed Taylor until he called her. And not seeing him for weeks had exacerbated the longing she'd continually denied acknowledging. There was something about her best friend's brother that turned her into an emotional pretzel whenever she asked herself what she wanted from Taylor and the answer continued to evade her.

Taylor's laugh caressed her ear. "Not hardly," he teased. "I'm calling to let you know I've leased a furnished condo for you less than ten miles from Bainbridge House, because the only extended-stay hotel was too far away. Your car is parked in the attached garage. Whenever you're ready, I'll pick you up and drive you back here."

"I'm ready now, Taylor. I just finished packing."

"How many bags do you have?"

"I have a Pullman, a smaller one with wheels and a carry-on bag with my laptop."

"I'll come up to your apartment and help you with your bags."

"That's not necessary. My uncle will help me."

"Are you sure?"

"Yes, Taylor. I'm sure."

"I'm on my way. I'll call you once I reach the bridge."

"Okay." Sonja wheeled her bags out of her bedroom to the entryway. She'd alerted her aunt and uncle days before that she would be leaving before the weekend.

Nelson pushed to his feet. "I guess this is it."

Sonja nodded. "Yes. But I'm not going down until Taylor calls to let me know he's on the GW Bridge."

Yolanda came out of the kitchen wiping her hands on a dish towel. "Don't get so involved in your work that you forget to take time to relax."

Sonja laughed. "I don't plan to work weekends." Taylor told her she was responsible for her own hours, and for her that meant taking Saturdays and Sundays off.

Yolanda approached Sonja and hugged her. "Good for you."

She returned her aunt's hug and kissed her cheek.

"I have some time before Taylor will be here to pick me up—I'll help you in the kitchen." Since she'd retired, Yolanda spent most of her time in the kitchen scrolling through the internet and trying out new recipes.

"I'm making your uncle's favorite. Puerto Rican lasagna."

"It's called *pastelón*."

Yolanda waved her hand. "It should be called *delicioso*, because the first time I tasted your mother's I've always wanted to make it. And this time I won't get a recipe from a book or the internet because Maria sent me her recipe."

"You're kidding? Mami never gives out her recipes." Sonja's grandmother had earned a reputation as one of the best cooks in her neighborhood and had passed her culinary skills onto her daughter.

Yolanda flashed a Cheshire cat grin. "I told her Nelson missed her *pastelón*. I wanted to know if she would send me her recipe. At first she said if he wanted some then all he had to do was drive up and she'd make a pan for him. When I opened my email to find the recipe, I had to assume she changed her mind."

"Lucky you."

"If you want, I'll forward a copy to you."

"*Gracias*, Titi."

Sonja sliced overripe plantains on a cutting board, making certain she yielded four slices per plantain and set them aside to be fried. The mouthwatering aroma of sautéed garlic and sofrito filled the kitchen, and she recalled the times when she'd sat on a stool watching her mother concoct the most delicious Caribbean-inspired dishes, and when older she became Maria's sous-chef. Sonja had inherited her love of cooking from her mother and grandmother, and she was looking forward to moving into the condo, where she could cook for herself.

When she got the call from Taylor that he was on the George Washington Bridge, Nelson helped her with her luggage, riding the elevator with her to the street level. "Will you get time off for a vacation?"

Sonja stared at Nelson as if he'd taken leave of his senses. She was only moving two—not two hundred—hours away. "Of course. If I decide to come home on a weekend, I'll call you beforehand." She did not want to remind Nelson that he played baseball with his retired buddies on Sundays, and when he wasn't playing ball he spent hours in front of the television watching whatever professional sport was in season.

She spied a gleaming silver SUV with Connecticut plates. "That's Taylor's Infiniti."

Nelson's eyebrows lifted. "Nice ride."

Taylor slowed and maneuvered next to a parked car. He tapped a button and the hatch opened. Sonja and the man he assumed was her uncle were wheeling the luggage to the rear of the Infiniti at the same time he got out. He took the handle of the Pullman from Sonja, lifting and placing it in the cargo area with the smaller suitcase and carry-on.

Smiling, he extended his hand to the slender middle-aged man. "Taylor Williamson."

Nelson stared at the proffered hand, and then took it. "Nelson Rios. Sonja's uncle. Make certain you take good care of my niece, Taylor Williamson."

"Tío!"

Taylor noticed the rush of color darkening Sonja's face. Her uncle had obviously embarrassed her. "It's okay, Sonja. Your uncle is just trying to protect you."

"I don't need protection," she snapped angrily. "Not from *any* man." Turning on her heel, she walked over to the passenger side of the Infiniti, got in and slammed the door harder than necessary.

Nelson threw up both hands. "What the hell did I say?"

"It must have been the wrong thing, for her to go off on you like that."

Nelson shook his head. "Tell her I'm sorry."

"I think it would be better if I don't say anything to her for a while." Taylor hadn't seen this side of Sonja, and instinct told him this wasn't the time to try to defend her uncle. "And I do want you to know that I intend to take good care of her."

Nelson nodded. "Thanks, son."

Taylor closed the hatch, then rounded the SUV and took his seat behind the wheel. He gave Sonja a sidelong glance as he fastened his seat belt. She was so still she could've been carved from stone and it was obvious she was in a funk. There was something about her expression that reminded him of Patrick's fiancée. Sonja was pouting like Andrea.

Well, Taylor mused, he wasn't his brother and Sonja wasn't his fiancée. He didn't have to plea and cajole her to talk to him, and there was nothing for which he had to apologize.

There was just the sound of the radio for nearly a half hour before he detected a grunt.

"Did you say something?"

"I said I don't need you to protect me."

Taylor's hands tightened on the steering wheel. "I didn't say I would protect you. It was your uncle asking that I take care of you. Try and see his side, Sonja. He sees you moving out and going away with a man he's never met and knows nothing about. That's what I call being concerned."

"I told him I would call and let him know where I'm staying."

"Why did you tell him that, Sonja?"

"Because he'd know where to contact me in case of an emergency."

"Couldn't he do that if he has your cell number?"

"Yes, but—"

"But nothing," Taylor interrupted. "Even if he didn't know your address, he could always track your cell. It's obvious the man loves you, but you failed to see the pain on his face when you screamed at him."

"I didn't scream at him."

"Yes, you did."

"Are you saying I should apologize to him?"

"It would behoove me not to tell you what to do. After all, you're a strong, independent, professional woman in control of her life and her destiny."

"Now you're being facetious, Taylor."

"Am I? Aren't you all of those adjectives?"

A beat passed. "I am."

"If you are, then own it, sweetheart."

Sonja met his eyes. "Do you realize this is the second time you've called me sweetheart."

"Really?" Taylor hadn't realized the endearment had just slipped out. And he had to ask himself if he wanted Sonja to be his sweetheart and the answer was a resounding yes. She was everything he liked in a woman. Her beauty aside, he was drawn to her intelligence and confidence.

"Yes, really, Taylor. Do you call all your women sweetheart?"

"No, because I don't have any women. I'm sorry, it was just a slip of the tongue."

"Apology accepted."

He couldn't tell Sonja that his father had always called his mother sweetheart and she probably would've thought it creepy that he was doing the same thing to her. As a young boy Taylor had been confused because he'd thought her name Elise, and when he'd asked Conrad why he'd called her that he said it was because she was the sweetest woman he'd ever known and he'd given her his heart.

Taylor recalled the time when he'd first come to

live with Conrad and Elise Williamson and found their behavior strange. He'd watched Conrad stare at his wife with what he would interpret once he entered adolescence as longing and lustful stares. Conrad would rest a hand at the small of her back, and when he suspected no one was looking, his hand would slip lower to cradle her hips. Blushing, Elise would whisper in his ear and he would remove his hand. He'd known his parents loved each other unconditionally and that love was transferred to the children they'd fostered and then legally adopted. Elise had always professed she would fight like a lioness protecting her cubs if anyone attempted to harm her children, and it was apparent her attitude was the same when she professed her displeasure toward Patrick's fiancée.

"Tell me about your parents," Sonja said after a comfortable silence.

Taylor wondered if Sonja could read his mind. "They were insanely in love," he said quietly after a moment. "I never heard my father raise his voice to my mother even when he was angry. He would walk away, leaving her talking to empty air. Then they would be lovey-dovey, acting as if nothing happened."

"Is that why you don't yell?"

"Yes, Sonja. Yelling and screaming never solves anything. What it does is make a bad situation worse and can only lead to unwarranted hostility."

Sonja locked eyes with him when he came to a

stop at a red light. "Are you talking about me and my uncle?"

"Yes. I think you misinterpreted what he'd said to me. What if I were a psychopath masquerading as an engineer to lure young women to a place where I'd torture and kill them?"

Sonja laughed. "It's apparent you watch shows depicting kidnapping, murder and mayhem."

"Don't laugh, Sonja, because it happens every day in every large and small city around the world."

"The difference is you're not a psychopath, and if you were then my former NYPD uncle and my active duty Special Forces brother would bypass the legal system and take you out."

"You wouldn't know that if you were dead. And maybe it was because your uncle was a cop and had taken the pledge to protect and serve that he felt the need to say what he did to me."

Sonja wanted to tell Taylor that he was being an alarmist, that she had nothing to fear from him. But when she thought about what her uncle had said to Taylor, she realized it was the first time Nelson had seen her with a man since she'd moved in with him and his wife. She hadn't revealed the intimate details of her failed marriage to anyone except Viola. She had trusted her friend to be neutral, unlike her father and brother, who probably would've confronted Hugh and made a bad situation worse. She'd told her parents that her marriage wasn't working because she'd felt like more of a daughter than a wife to her much older husband, and decided to file for divorce.

"You're probably right about my uncle."

"I know I'm right."

"I suppose I should call him and apologize."

"I agree."

"There's no need for you to act so smug, Taylor," she countered. "I'll have to call him later because I put my cell phone in the carry-on bag."

Taylor tapped the navigation screen. "My number is synced to Bluetooth. You can call him from here."

She tapped in Nelson's number. It rang twice before he picked up. "What's the matter?"

Sonja registered fear in her uncle's strident query. "Nothing is the matter, *tío*. I'm using Taylor's cell because mine is in one of the bags. I'm calling to apologize for screaming at you. I'm sorry I overreacted."

"There's no need to apologize, *muñeca*. I've forgotten about it."

"Well, if you have, then it is the same with me. *Te quiero*."

"Yo también te quiero."

"What does *muñeca* mean?" Taylor asked after she'd ended the call.

"Doll. My uncle has always called me that."

"Would it bother you if I called you *muñeca*?"

"What happened to sweetheart?" she teased, smiling.

"What if I use them interchangeably?"

Sonja sobered because she felt they were about to

embark on something neither needed nor possibly wanted. Especially not her. She couldn't afford to become involved with someone she had to see and work with every day. Taylor Williamson was too potent a man for her to completely ignore. There were times when he looked at her and she felt as if he could see beyond the wall she'd erected to keep men out of her life; that her lips professed one thing while her celibate body screamed for her to sleep with a man, if only to assuage the frustration she'd denied for far too long. She'd filled her spare time with work, reading romance novels and watching television programming dedicated to love and romance. And she'd been successful until coming face-to-face with her best friend's brother.

Even if she was able to dismiss his gorgeous face and body, it was his soothing and calming voice, intelligence and down-to-earth personality that drew her in and refused to let her go. And his wealth never factored into the equation that he was a certified trifecta.

At that moment Sonja realized she was tired. Tired of pretending that she did not need a man, when she wanted a relationship where she was treated as an equal and not an ornament or trophy taken out and put on display whenever it suited her partner. Taylor had offered to be her friend, and not seeing him for many weeks made her aware that she wanted more than friendship. And she knew she had to be the first to thrown down the gauntlet to ascertain whether he would be receptive.

"It wouldn't bother me if you called me doll or sweetheart." She knew she'd shocked him when his foot suddenly hit the brake, the SUV coming to a complete stop in the middle of the street, followed by a cacophony of blaring horns. Her heart was pumping a runaway rhythm when she realized they could've been rear-ended by the car behind them. "Taylor, you're holding up traffic."

He eased off the brake and resumed driving. He took his right hand off the wheel and covered her left, resting on her thigh, brought it to his mouth and kissed the back of it. "I believe we're going to have a lot of fun working together."

Sonja had fought the dynamic vitality he'd exuded effortlessly and failed. "You think?"

Taylor winked at her. "I know."

He'd said the two words with such confidence that it buoyed hers. They had time, at least a year, to discover where their friendship would take them.

Chapter Seven

With wide eyes, Sonja stared at the gatehouse. "Isn't this where your mother lives?" she asked Taylor. He'd told her his mother owned a condo in a gated community.

"No. Her condo is in Sparta. It's about thirteen miles south of here."

Taylor decelerated and then came to a complete stop at the gatehouse. He lowered the driver's-side window and spoke to the man inside the enclosure. She couldn't hear what they were saying. The attendant leaned down and peered in at Sonja. Smiling, he waved to her, and she returned his wave with one of her own.

The gate rose smoothly, and Taylor drove through,

following a paved road to an enclave of two-story farmhouse structures with broad porches, second-floor balconies and attached garages. There were signposts along the road indicating the direction to shops, the recreation center, movie theater and restaurant.

"How did you find this place?" Sonja asked.

"I contacted a Realtor, who told me the developer was having a problem selling units, and rather than leave them vacant he'd opted to lease a few. From what I've seen of the development I think you'll enjoy living here."

"I like what I see. It appears I won't have to leave to shop for food or eat out." She paused. "Do you know why it has been difficult to sell all the units?"

"Personally, I believe even with the number of on-site amenities they're overpriced. Folks could buy a four- or five-bedroom home in the Poconos built on half an acre for a lot less than these two- and three-bedrooms."

"How much does a three-bedroom go for?"

"Why? Are you thinking of buying one?"

Sonja shook her head. "Not hardly. If I was going to purchase property, it wouldn't be in the middle of nowhere even with on-site amenities. However, if I were looking to downsize later in life, then maybe I would consider it."

"Are you saying you couldn't see yourself living at Bainbridge House?"

"I could if I was a docent."

Taylor pulled into the driveway to a house at the end of a street and shut off the engine. "Bainbridge House is not going to be a museum."

Shifting on her seat, Sonja turned and gave Taylor a long, penetrating stare. "It could be a hotel *and* a museum. I told you before that I have some ideas about the property, so if you want we can talk about it after I settle in."

Taylor unsnapped his belt. "Okay. Why don't you take a few days to get used to your surroundings before you begin working."

"What are you going to do?"

"I've scheduled interviews for several days this week."

She nodded. "I'd like to ask a favor."

"What's that?"

"I'd like to go through the trunks during my downtime."

"You want me to bring them here?"

"Yes."

"Are you sure, Sonja?"

"Yes, I am sure." She had carefully enunciated each word. "After spending hours attempting to identify the period and style of a particular plate, fork or candlestick, examining the contents of the trunks will be like a breath of fresh air." Sonja didn't tell Taylor that she was curious to uncover additional information about the original owners of the historic house. Old letters, journals, bills of sale were helpful when authenticating items.

"I'll bring them over later tonight."

She inclined her head. "Thank you, sir."

Taylor smiled. "You're welcome, ma'am. Let's go inside so you can check out your new digs.

Sonja stared, tongue-tied, as she surveyed the open floor plan of the house that was to become a place she could call home. White walls, with creamy upholstered furniture, heightened the illusion of openness in the living, dining, and family rooms, which made the space appear even larger. White cabinets, yellow and cornflower blue tiles, and cobalt blue countertops and colorful accessories created a cheerful mood in the contemporary kitchen. The classic combination of blue and white was timeless and was repeated in throw pillows, area rugs and the dining area chair seat cushions.

Looking over her shoulder, she smiled at Taylor. "It's perfect. Thank you." And for Sonja it *was* perfect. Move-in ready with a large wall-mounted television and audio components in the family room and under-cabinet radio in the kitchen.

He moved closer and put an arm around her waist. "I was hoping you would like it."

"Of course, I like it."

"It's one of two two-bedroom model units."

Moving into the condo would signal a significant change in Sonja's life. It would be the first time in twenty years she would live independently of others. First, she'd lived on base with her parents; then she'd shared an off-campus apartment with a roommate before marrying Hugh and moving into his house. During their separation she'd gone from her husband's house to her parents' retirement home in the Adirondack Mountains to heal and plan the next phase of what had been her tumultuous life. And once she decided to return to college, it wasn't in Boston, but in New York City, where she'd moved in with her aunt and uncle.

Taylor kissed her hair. "I'm going back to the car to bring your bags in."

"And I'm going upstairs to see the rest of the place."

Sonja felt as if she was walking on air as she climbed the staircase to the second story. The condo contained two bedrooms: one master and another smaller one she could use as an office. The master had a sitting area and an en suite bath. She thought of the bedroom as a romantic retreat with voluminous pale silk drapes covering floor-to-ceiling windows and sliding doors with built-in blinds that opened out to the balcony. She focused her attention on a king-size four-poster mahogany bed. The bed linens, with layers of pillows in differing patterns, repeated the first floor's blue-and-white palette. A creamy-white armchair with a matching footstool, close to a small round mahogany table in the seating area, was the perfect place for her to kick back and relax before retiring for bed.

Sonja left the master suite and walked into the bedroom across the hall, wondering if Taylor had chosen this unit because he'd believed she would like the colors and furnishings. Suddenly she recalled his preference for blues and grays while she preferred earth tones. Had he, she mused, selected this unit because of his affinity for blue? She recalled the exquisitely tailored royal blue suit he'd worn during their initial meeting at The Cellar.

The decorating style in the smaller bedroom was Swedish country with wood furniture painted in tones of white. The decorator differed from the classic approach by including French provincial and country influences. Duvets in a toile de Jouy pattern covered twin beds with off-white headboards, and white linens and a crocheted bed skirt beneath the duvets artfully corroborated the Swedish theme of elegant white. A table and chair next to a blue-and-white-checkered upholstered chair and ottoman would do double duty as her desk. Sonja had walked out of the bedroom when she spied Taylor coming up the staircase carrying her Pullman.

He had removed a sweatshirt to reveal a tee stamped with a college logo; it hugged his muscular upper body like second skin, and her mouth went dry when Sonja realized she was lusting after a man with whom she would have to work closely over the next year. And she didn't need anyone to tell her that she was being a hypocrite. Taylor was her boss and he'd offered friendship, but for Sonja that wasn't enough. She wanted more and the more translated into what had been missing in her life even before she'd con-

sidered ending her marriage: intimacy. The very no-
tion of her wanting to sleep with Taylor shook her
to the core.

"Where do you want me to put this?" Taylor asked
her.

She blinked slowly as if coming out of a trance.
"You can put it in the master. I'll go and get the
other bags."

"Don't bother. I'll bring them up."

She wasn't about to argue with him. "I'm going
downstairs to get my cell and bag from the carry-
on. Then you can put it in the other bedroom." Sonja
knew she had to put some space between them for
a few minutes if only to regain control of her fragile emotions.

Smiling, Taylor executed a snappy salute. "Okay,
boss lady."

"Yeah, right," she drawled, trying not to smile.
Sonja discovered the two bags at the foot of the staircase and removed her cell phone and cross-body
from the carry-on.

Taylor returned and hoisted the two bags, his bi-
ceps bulging from the exertion. "After I come down
I'll give you a key card for the house, fob for your car
and the corporate credit card. I'll hang onto the extra
key card and fob in case you either lose or misplace
them. There's a remote device under the visor that
will allow you access at the gatehouse."

Sonja nodded. She wanted to tell Taylor she'd
never lost or misplaced her keys, but if it made him

feel more secure then she wasn't going to argue with him. Walking into the kitchen, she opened the French-door refrigerator. It was empty except for a box of baking soda. Sonja opened the cabinets, finding them empty, and then a door in a far corner of the kitchen and discovered a pantry and half bathroom. A stackable washer and dryer were set up behind café doors.

She detected movement behind her and turned to find Taylor standing only feet away. Her heartbeat kicked into a higher gear.

"You can't do that," she said in a breathless whisper.

"Do what?"

"Sneak up on me."

Crossing muscular arms over his chest, Taylor smiled at her. "Sorry about that. Next time I'll make some noise."

Sonja blew out a breath. "Thanks. I need to go food shopping to stock the fridge and the pantry, and also buy plates, cups, glasses and flatware."

Taylor held out his hand. "Come with me. I have to pull my car out the driveway before you can get yours out of the garage."

"What did you get me?"

He winked at her. "You'll see."

Sonja doubled over laughing hysterically when Taylor tapped the button on the automatic garage opener and she saw the vehicle he'd leased for her.

It was an Infiniti QX50—the smallest model of the QX SUVs.

"I can't believe you got the same style and color as yours."

"When you admired mine, I thought I'd get you the smaller version."

"Thank you." The two words sounded empty to Sonja once she realized Taylor was thinking about her when he had made the decision to lease the SUV. "I really appreciate the thought, Taylor."

He handed her the fob. "Anything to make the lives of my team easier. You're going to have your work cut out for you once you begin going through those crates. What you saw in the cellar wasn't even half of what has been stored there."

Sonja went still. "What are you talking about?"

"The maintenance people discovered a door to a storeroom hidden behind several armoires. The space is filled with as many crates as what you saw."

"Oh no!"

"Oh yes," Taylor said, smiling. "I didn't even bother to look at what was written on them—I just closed the door."

"Your ancestors probably were hoarders."

"Either hoarders, collectors or packrats."

Sonja was tempted to mention the museum again to Taylor but held her tongue. Bainbridge House was large enough to operate as a hotel, wedding venue *and* a museum. "Let me get my bag with my license so I can drive Silver Bullet to see if she purrs or roars."

Taylor ran a hand over his cropped hair. "Please don't tell me you just named your car."

"Of course. Doesn't yours have a name?"

"Yeah. QX80."

She made a sucking sound with her tongue and teeth. "That's the model number."

"Well, that's what it is."

"Well, my new baby is Silver Bullet."

Taylor shook his head. "Go get your bag, Sonja."

Sonja adjusted the seat to accommodate her shorter legs, tapped the start-engine button and slowly backed out of the garage. It was a while since she'd been behind the wheel, and this was her first time driving a sport utility vehicle.

"How does it feel?" Taylor asked. He sat in the passenger seat as she drove slowly in the direction of the business area.

"Nice, even though I'm not used to sitting up this high. I think I'm going to enjoy driving on the parkways." She came to a complete stop at a stop sign, then continued, not exceeding the posted fifteen miles per hour.

Sonja drove into the lot behind the strip mall, parking near the supermarket. The condos may have been overpriced, but for her the trade-off was convenience. She was certain to patronize the hair and nail salon, variety store, dry cleaner and restaurant.

"I'm going to the variety store to pick up some housewares." Not only did she need pots, pans and dishes, flatware and serving pieces, but also linens, kitchen and bath towels, and a laundry basket.

Taylor nodded. "I'll meet you in the supermarket. You said you need to stock the pantry, so I figured I'd pick up canned goods and nonperishables."

"Okay."

She peered into his cart near to overflowing with cans of beans and other vegetables, boxes of pasta, rice, sugar, flour, vinegar, cooking and olive oil, and a variety of cleaning supplies. "You did good."

"Thank you, sweetheart. What's for dinner?"

Sonja gave him a level look. "You want me to cook for you?"

"Yes. If you cook for me tomorrow night, then I'll return the favor and cook for you the following day."

"You cook?"

"Duh! Who do you think feeds me?"

Sonja felt as if she'd suddenly come down with a case of foot-in-mouth. She didn't know why she'd assumed Taylor was unable to prepare a meal for himself. "All right," she said, hoping to cover up her faux pas.

"What are you making?"

"I don't know. I'll think about it once we get home."

Once we get home.

Taylor repeated the four words to himself. Had

Sonja actually thought of the condo as theirs? When he was shown the two model units he'd purposely selected the one with the cheerful blue-and-white furnishings because he felt it complemented Sonja's romantic nature. She'd admitted she read romance novels and watched Hallmark movies.

Taylor knew he'd been lying to himself for weeks. He'd almost convinced himself that there could never be more between him and Sonja Rios-Martin than friendship. Even though he'd told himself that over and over, he knew it was a lie, and he'd purposely kept his distance, hoping his feelings for her would translate into out of sight, out of mind. But even that had proved unsuccessful.

There was something about his sister's friend that was so different from any other woman with whom he'd been involved. Sonja wasn't reticent when it came to speaking her mind, and that meant he did not have to guess what she was thinking or attempt to interpret something she'd said. She was intelligent, poised and confident, qualities he admired most in a woman. Then there was her sensual beauty. Just looking at her, inhaling the intoxicating scent of her perfume, touching her hand or a part of her body, and the husky quality of her voice he never tired of listening to. The only thing missing was how she tasted. Taylor longed to kiss her sexy mouth with a need bordering on obsession, and it had taken all his self-control not to act on his fantasy.

144 *A NEW FOUNDATION*

"You can ring up these two carts together," he told the register clerk.

He emptied his cart, bagging everything. And then he bagged the items in Sonja's cart. He handed the checker a credit card. Between him and Sonja they'd bought enough food to last her for several weeks. He took the receipt and returned the card to a case in the pocket of his jeans.

"Let's go, *muñeca*," he said, grinning and winking at Sonja.

"I'm ready whenever you are, *papi*."

His eyebrows shot up. He'd lost count of the number of times he'd heard Spanish-speaking girls call their boyfriends *papi*, and it was always said as a term of affection. Taylor pushed his cart and pulled Sonja's as he followed her to the SUV.

"So, I'm your *papi*?"

"Only if you want to be."

Taylor stopped and met her eyes. "I do." The two words were firm, final, and in that instant he knew he and Sonja had silently acknowledged both were open to see where their friendship would lead. "What on earth did you buy?" he asked, moving the bags behind the rear seats to make room for the contents of the shopping carts.

"Pots, pans, dishes, sheets, towels, small appliances and other knickknacks for the kitchen and bathrooms. I also bought a single-serve coffeemaker and an electric kettle, because I need my coffee in the morning and chamomile tea at night."

He gave her a sidelong glance as she handed him

bags from the carts. "Do you have a problem going to sleep?"

"Sometimes. But that's only when I'm overthinking something."

"I hope that doesn't happen when you begin working. I've told you I have a two-year timeline in which to fully restore the house and property. Even though you have a lot to appraise and catalogue I don't want you stressed out about it. You can set your own hours and at no time will you be obligated to check with me unless you have a question or problem. I'll have enough to do, working with the contractors and making certain I don't incur too many cost overruns. I don't want too many verbal rounds with my brother."

"Do you have a final budget for the entire project?"

"Not yet. Patrick has been adjusting the budget for the house as needed. He has one for the château, one for the outbuildings, including the cottages, stables and barn, and another for the gardens, golf course, reflecting pools and fountains. Why did you ask?"

"I haven't seen the entire property, but based on restoration projects I've observed in France and Italy I guesstimate it will cost you between ninety and one hundred million dollars."

"That sounds about right," Taylor said, neither confirming nor denying the dollar amount.

"Sounds about right, Taylor?"

Taylor knew it was impossible to deceive Sonja. "You're right. How did you know?"

"I know you're going to have to hire electricians, plumbers, roofers, carpenters, stonemasons, and landscape architects. Faux bois specialists are necessary to restore the walls in the library and the moldings in the ballrooms. A cleaning crew and exterminators also factor into the cost along with workers needed to haul away debris. Replacement doors and windows will have to be ordered from Italy, and if there's a need to replace roof tiles, I can give you the name of a Vermont quarry that can ship them to you."

Taylor wanted to ask Sonja how she knew the doors and windows had come from Italy. Did she only have to glance at an object to ascertain its origin? "You're going to prove invaluable and an essential member of the restoration team."

"I hope so."

"I know so, Sonja—otherwise I never would've hired you."

"I thought you hired me because Viola pressured you to."

He blinked slowly. "Is that really what you think?"

"I don't know, Taylor. You tell me. You didn't believe me when I told you I was an architectural historian?"

"I believed you because Viola, who rarely gives out compliments, said you're a genius when it comes to identifying antiques. When Patrick asked for letters of recommendation and I told him I would vouch for you, it had nothing to do with Viola singing your praises. I don't have time to look for another architectural historian so, regardless of what you think or believe, you're it, Sonja."

A mysterious smile parted her lips. "Are you saying we're a good combination?"

"Yeah. Like peanut butter and jelly," Taylor said teasingly.

"No, Taylor. Like shrimp and grits."

"Nice. But how about bacon and eggs?"

She scrunched up her nose as she handed him another bag. "I've got one better. Chicken and waffles."

"Hell, yeah! I've got a special recipe for chicken and waffles, and one of these days I'm going to make them for you."

"I usually have chicken and waffles along with mimosas for Sunday brunch."

Taylor closed the door to the hatch. "I suppose that means I'll have to come over one Sunday morning and put my money where my mouth is."

Sonja bit her lip, bringing his gaze to linger on her mouth. "We will see."

"Yes, we will. If you don't mind, I'd like to drive Silver Bullet back to the house," Taylor volunteered.

"I don't mind since you acknowledged her correctly."

Cupping Sonja's elbow, he steered her around to the passenger side, opened the door and assisted her up. Taylor stared up at her. "If you had to name my vehicle, what would it be?"

"Gray Wolf."

Taylor angled his head. "I like that. Gray Wolf it is. After I help you put everything away, I'm going up to the house to get the trunks and copies I made of the blueprints and floor plans. By the way, the papers are wrapped in oilskin, which has preserved them from moisture and rot, and the floor plans and blueprints have been stored in metal tubes."

"Bring them by tomorrow. I need to unpack and put everything away."

"I have morning meetings, so I probably won't be able to come over until late afternoon," Taylor said.

"That'll work. Don't forget I'm making dinner."

He wanted to tell Sonja there was no way he would forget. "Do you want me to bring anything?"

"No. I think I have everything I need."

Taylor drove back to the condo, and he and Sonja made quick work of unloading the bags and carrying them to the kitchen. "Do you need help putting things away?"

Sonja shook her head. "I don't think so."

"It looks as if you're really going to be busy, so why don't we put off sharing dinner for a couple of days."

"That's not necessary. I'm going to stay up tonight and finish everything."

"So, we're still on for tomorrow night?" he asked. "Yes."

Taking a step, Taylor lowered his head and brushed a light kiss over her parted lips. "I'll see you tomorrow." He knew he'd shocked her when he heard her hushed gasp.

Turning on his heel, he left the kitchen and walked out to where he'd parked his vehicle.

Chapter Eight

Taylor tapped a button on the steering wheel, increasing the radio's volume as he sang to Bruno Mars's "Uptown Funk." Knowing he was going to share dinner with Sonja put him in a party mood. It had been impulsive when he'd invited himself to her home and then asked if she would cook for him.

And if he were honest with himself he would have to admit he had been intrigued before Sonja introduced herself to him at The Cellar. When Viola called her from his car, putting their conversation on speaker he'd been mesmerized with the timbre of her voice. And the expression on her face when he opened the garage door to reveal the vehicle he'd leased for her was imprinted on his memory like a permanent tattoo. It was a combination of shock and then pure joy. It had been the same when she'd walked into the condo. She may have thought of them as perks, but he viewed them as necessities to make her life less stressful and had given her the option of setting her own hours. He did not relish the task of going through hundreds of crates, examining each item and cataloguing or authenticating it as an antique or a reproduction.

Taylor lowered the volume on the radio when a familiar name appeared on the navigation screen. "What's up, stranger?"

"That's what I should be asking you, Williamson."

"It's all good, Robbie. Right now I'm living the dream."

"I'm glad you are because I'm so sick and tired of Lansing, Allen and Payette's dog-and-pony show that I'm seriously thinking about walking into HR and quitting, but not before giving them the middle finger."

Taylor smothered a laugh even though what Robinson Harris had said was no laughing matter. After the company's merger several years back things began to change. It was gradual at first, but after a number of Payette's board members gained a monopoly, the entire culture of the company changed—and not positively. Layoffs escalated, salaries and promotions were frozen, and supervisors were told to lean heavily on their workers to complete construction projects before the designated date in order to maximize profits.

"I'm sorry I didn't get back to you sooner, but I just got the message. Kendall took my phone when we broke up. She only gave it back once she'd let me into her apartment to get my things. In the interim I was using a prepaid phone."

Taylor suspected the woman in Robinson Harris's life had tired of being his girlfriend when she'd hinted to Taylor that she wanted to become Mrs. Harris. "I'm sorry to hear that."

"It's okay. I'm over it."

Taylor wanted to ask him how he could be over a woman he'd dated for more than two years. He wasn't calling Robinson about his love life but about whether he wanted to work for him as his project manager. He was a brilliant architectural engineer who had been passed over for a promised promotion before the merger.

"Do you want to leave the dog-and-pony show?"

There was complete silence from the other end of the connection. "You know I do."

"I just might make that a reality if you agree to come and work for me."

"For you and not with you? What are you into, Williamson?"

Taylor chuckled softly. "Why do you make it sound as if I'm involved in some shady business?"

"Are you?"

"Hell, no! I'm working with my family, and we'll need a project manager for the next two years."

Taylor made certain to say *we* rather than *I*. Although he'd supervise the restoration of the house and outbuildings, his brothers and sister had their assigned tasks before Bainbridge House was approved to operate as a hotel and wedding venue.

"You want me to come and work with you?"

"That's why I called you, Robbie." Taylor told him about the project and how he had set aside several weeks in which to interview licensed general contractors. "If you're interested I'd like you to come up and see what I am talking about."

"When can you make time for me?" Robbie asked.

"Next week. I'll let you know when I can block out time to spend the entire day with you."

"Where is the property?" Robbie asked.

"North Jersey."

"I'm familiar with the area because my sister lives in Hackettstown."

"Good. I'll talk to you later."

"Taylor?"

Taylor was taken aback—Robbie had always called him by his surname. "Yes."

"Even if you don't hire me, I want to thank you for thinking of me."

"You misunderstood me, Robbie. I do want to hire you."

"If you want me, then I'm your man."

"I'll be in touch."

When he'd called Robbie and hadn't heard from him, Taylor didn't know what to make of it. It wasn't like his friend not to return his call, and now he knew why. If his former coworker was willing to accept the position as project manager, then he would have filled the two most important positions.

Sonja had mentioned hiring faux bois specialists to restore the walls and moldings, and he planned to give her the responsibility of finding them. Once Robbie came on board, together they would examine the château's foundation to make certain it was stable before any work began.

He also thought about what Sonja had said about ordering windows and doors from Italy and roof tiles from a Vermont quarry. The latter was more easily obtainable than the imported items. If he wasn't able to get the windows installed before the cold weather, then they would have to wait until the following spring.

Taylor had given himself a two-year window in which to refurbish the château, barn, stables, and cottages, to take undue pressure off himself and everyone else involved.

Within that time frame Joaquin would've fulfilled his contracts and could begin to redesign the gardens, and Tariq could purchase horses for the stables.

A sixth sense told him that Viola would eventually supervise the kitchen because she'd never been one to let her brothers exclude her from any of their joint plans. And he was okay with Patrick's role as

CFO of the foundation, because no one else would monitor the bottom line like his certified accountant brother.

Conrad had made Elise promise to carry out his wish to restore his ancestral home, and Taylor had promised his mother he would see it to fruition.

Sonja checked the dining area table for what seemed the umpteenth time before realizing old habits die hard. She'd set the table for two with cloth napkins, water goblets, wineglasses and a vase of daisies as the centerpiece. She had also lit jars of scented candles and set them on tables in the living and family rooms.

As Hugh's wife, she had presided over so many dinner parties that one blended into the next until she'd lost count of how many she'd hosted in the four years they'd lived together. Her then mother-in-law would come by and check on how she'd set the table, and then lecture her in a too-sweet soft voice that a spoon or fork wasn't in its proper place. After a while she'd come to resent the presence of the passive-aggressive woman who doted on her only son.

It was only after Sonja freed herself of the invisible shackles of her husband and mother-in-law that she had come to the realization that Hugh hated his controlling mother, but rather than confront her as a fortysomething-year-old adult, he'd transferred his resentment onto his wife. The day Sonja worked up the courage to put whatever she could carry in a bag and climb into the back seat of a taxi to take her to the nearest bus station was the moment she'd taken control of her life. She had boarded a bus from Boston to Burlington, Vermont, where she checked into a motel for the night. The next day she'd called her mother let her know she'd left her husband and asked her to take the ferry and pick her up. Within minutes of the ferry docking and her mother alighting from the car Sonja did something she rarely did. She cried. Somehow she'd worked up the nerve to free herself from a man who'd controlled every aspect of her life from morning to night. Her mother also cried when she saw her because Sonja was a former shadow of herself. She had lost weight she could ill afford to lose. It taken her nearly a month to plot her escape, and during that time she had been so stressed out that Hugh would uncover her plan that she found it hard to eat more than a few forkfuls of food at any given time. And if Hugh noticed her weight loss, he did not mention it because of his preference for waiflike models.

And that night, once she'd settled into the guest bedroom at her parents' lakefront home, Sonja cried inconsolably. While the tears were cathartic, it would be a long time before she'd completely rid herself of the man. In her naïveté she had replaced her father with Hugh. He'd initially been her protector, but whenever she sought to exercise a modicum of independence he'd quickly quash it. Sonja had overlooked it until it was apparent he did not want to be challenged but obeyed, without her questioning his motives. He'd referred to her as his "little wife," and that was what she'd become because it was easier to acquiesce than argue with him.

Sonja shook her head as if to rid it of her past. It was now time for her to concentrate on the present and her future. When she awoke earlier that morning she'd found herself completely disoriented, and it had taken a full minute before she realized where she was. She knew she wasn't in her regular bedroom because of the sunlight coming in through the windows. Her Inwood apartment had southern exposure, and the sun didn't fill the space until the afternoon. She'd lie in bed, staring up at the ceiling waiting for the butterflies in her stomach to go away, because at that moment she was a butterfly emerging from the cocoon and becoming free—freer than she'd ever been in her life.

Sonja hadn't realized it until now, but Taylor Williamson had become the hero in one of her romance novels. He unknowingly had offered her something she wasn't consciously aware that she needed—independence.

Once she knew Taylor had hired her, she'd called her mother to let her about her new position and that she would have to take up residence in a hotel to be closer to the work site. Maria congratulated her, while reminding Sonja that she was entitled to every good thing coming her way because she'd worked for it. Sonja knew her mother was talking about overcoming a toxic marriage to return to college to complete the courses needed to become an architectural historian.

She smiled. It had taken twenty-four hours for Sonja to fall in love with her new home. All of the units were connected; however, fenced-in backyards provided privacy from her nearest neighbors. The second-story balcony was the perfect spot for her to sit and enjoy her morning coffee, while offering unrestricted panoramic views of a forested area in the distance. She was looking forward to witnessing the change of seasons. The master bathroom had a soaking tub, oversize shower stall with twin showerheads and a double vanity. This would be her personal retreat, where she could spend as much time as she wanted without someone knocking on the door to ask when she was coming out. Her uncle's two-bedroom apartment had only one bathroom.

The kitchen was a cook's dream—eye-level ovens with a warming drawer, microwave, double sinks, and a stovetop with six burners and a grill. The built-in refrigerator and freezer was large enough to store meat and perishables for months at a time.

The intercom buzzed, startling Sonja as she glanced at the clock on the microwave. It was minutes before six o'clock. Taylor had sent her a text indicating he would arrive at her house around six. Walking over to the wall, she tapped the button.

"Yes?"

"This is the gatehouse. There's a Mr. Williamson here to see you."

"Please let him in."

She didn't know why he'd asked to be announced when he had a remote device that would allow him access onto the property. Leaving the kitchen, she walked to the door and opened the inner one. Her pulse quickened when she saw Taylor get out of his vehicle and walk around to the rear. He removed a hand truck and loaded it with two steamer trunks. With wide eyes, she stared at the logo on the luxury beige and brown trunks. The monogram with quatrefoils, flowers and LV were recognizable as the Louis Vuitton brand. He balanced another carton on top of the trunks.

She opened the outer door and allowed Taylor to enter. The familiar fragrance of his cologne wafted to her nostrils as he moved past her. He'd exchanged his ubiquitous jeans, tees or sweatshirts, and boots for a pale blue linen shirt, navy slacks and black leather slip-ons. Her heart rate kicked into a higher gear when he smiled at her. It was the same apparent smirk he'd affected when modeling. It seemed to say I see you looking at me, and do you like what you see?

Hell, yeah, her inner voice said. Not only did she like what she saw, she also liked him. Sonja knew she had to stop denying that she liked and wanted Taylor for more than friendship. She'd had a few guy friends before and after her marriage, and now it was time for her to acknowledge that she wanted a relationship with someone willing to accept her and her imperfections, and for her it would be the same with him. Sonja wasn't looking or asking for declarations of love, but rather respect. She wanted and needed a man to respect her and for him to treat her as his equal.

"Do you still want me to take the trunks upstairs?" Taylor asked, hoping Sonja didn't notice the huskiness in his voice. He'd promised her they would remain friends, but now he wasn't certain he would be able to keep his promise.

Sonja nodded. "Yes. I can't believe someone would use luxury trunks rather than file cabinets to store paperwork. If I wanted to buy one of these today, the price tag would be more than forty thousand."

"That's crazy," Taylor spit out. "I'd rather donate forty thousand dollars to my favorite charities instead of a single piece of luggage."

"You're preaching to the choir, Taylor."

He gave her a narrow look. "How do you know the price tag?"

"I spent a month in Italy on holiday at the beginning of the year. Instead of going to museums, I spent most of my time eating in restaurants off the beaten track and browsing through countless shops. There is a Vuitton shop in Milan's Galleria Vittorio Emanuele II. That's where I saw the trunks. I was told if I live in the States and wanted to purchase one, then it would be a special order."

He slowly shook his head. "No, thank you."

Taylor tried not to stare at Sonja and failed miserably. He couldn't pull his gaze away from the wealth of curls framing her face and ending above her shoulders. When he'd met her at The Cellar he'd thought of her a seductress in red. If he had to give her a label, then it would be chameleon. She was able to smoothly transition from a seductress in red with a profusion of waves framing her face and makeup accentuating her best features to a fresh-faced ingenue while affecting a ponytail, jeans and running shoes. Tonight she'd changed again when she'd selected a tangerine-orange sheath dress, black ballet flats and a subtle hint of makeup. Smoky taupe shadow on her lids complemented her large brown eyes, and the orange lip color contrasted beautifully with the gold undertones in her complexion. And her curly hairstyle reminded him of a doll—the nickname with which her uncle had tagged her.

He set the carton of wine on the floor and sniffed the air, smiling. "Something smells delicious."

Sonja closed the door, locking it, and then flashed a mysterious smile. "I know how much you liked the dishes at La Casa Del Mofongo, so I decided to make *arroz blanco*, *frijoles rosados, pollo asado* and flan for dessert."

"I understood flan, and that's about it. And I'm

FREE BOOKS GIVEAWAY

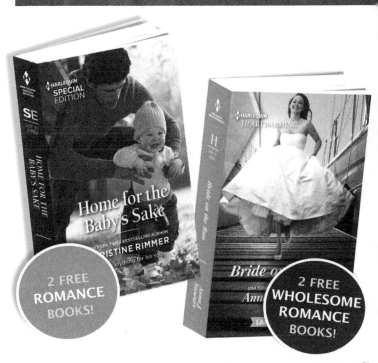

Complete the survey below and return it today to receive up to 4 FREE BOOKS and FREE GIFTS guaranteed!

FREE BOOKS GIVEAWAY
Reader Survey

1
Do you prefer stories with happy endings?

○ YES   ○ NO

2
Do you share your favorite books with friends?

○ YES   ○ NO

3
Do you often choose to read instead of watching TV?

○ YES   ○ NO

YES! Please send me my Free Rewards, consisting of **2 Free Books from each series I select** and **Free Mystery Gifts**. I understand that I am under no obligation to buy anything, as explained on the back of this card.

❏ **Harlequin® Special Edition** (235/335 HDL GQ2U)
❏ **Harlequin® Heartwarming™ Larger-Print** (161/361 HDL GQ2U)
❏ **Try Both** (235/335 & 161/361 HDL GQ26)

FIRST NAME

LAST NAME

ADDRESS

APT.#

CITY

STATE/PROV.

ZIP/POSTAL CODE

EMAIL ❏ Please check this box if you would like to receive newsletters and promotional emails from Harlequin Enterprises ULC and its affiliates. You can unsubscribe anytime.

SE/HW-820-FBG21

not ashamed to say that I could eat Spanish food every day."

"I'm serving white rice, pink beans and roast chicken. Instead of a salad, I've decided to prepare a cheese and fruit platter. By the way, have you ever eaten *pastelón*?"

He shook his head. I don't think so. What is it?"

"Puerto Rican lasagna. My mother gave my aunt the recipe and she in turn gave it to me. I'll make it for you one of these days."

"I suppose I'm going to have to up my game when cooking for you."

Sonja rested her hands at her waist. "Are you talking about a throwdown, Taylor?"

"Not quite. But I can't have you show me up."

"Who taught you to cook?"

"My mother. In fact, she taught all of her children because she claimed once we left home she wanted us to be totally independent, and for her that translated into the ability to put a meal on the table." He paused. "I'm going to take these trunks upstairs, then we can talk about cooking for each other."

Taylor pulled the stair-climbing hand truck up the staircase and down the hallway to the smaller bedroom Sonja had claimed as her office. He noticed she had already put her personal touch on the space. She'd placed a laptop and printer on the desk, and framed photos occupied every flat surface. He peered closely at one with Sonja, her brother and her parents when she'd graduated college. There were others of her uncle, brother and father in uniform. Then there was another one with Sonja holding a baby in a christening gown. Not only was she *titi*, she was also a godmother. He left the trunks on the floor next to the desk, returned to the first floor and joined Sonja in the kitchen.

"It looks as if you've done more shopping." Bottles of red, white and rosé were stored in a wine rack on the countertop.

Sonja turned and smiled at Taylor over her shoulder. "Yes, I did. Thank you for the wine. I didn't know whether you were bringing anything." Not only had she visited the wine shop, but also the florist and a craft shop where she'd purchased scented candles, bundles of potpourri and framed prints with pressed leaves and flowers for the bathrooms. She'd also stopped at the variety store to pick up an ample supply of paper clips, folders, notebooks, legal pads, rubber bands, sticky notes, a stapler, tape and a desk organizer caddy.

"I must admit your house now looks like a home."

Sonja met his eyes. "It's the little touches that make a house a home." The supermarket had a section with plants and live flowers, and she'd selected a combination of potted ferns and succulents.

"You've done well, Sonja."

She affected a graceful curtsy. "Thank you."

Taylor winked at her. "You're welcome. I'm going to put the case of wine in the pantry, then I'm going to wash my hands."

"I'd also bought a case. It looks as if we have enough to last for a while."

"Don't forget, you're going to live here for at least the next two years."

"You're right, Taylor."

Sonja wanted to ask Taylor if she would be obligated to stay if she completed her project before the lease expired. Would he allow her to continue to live in the condo, or would she be forced to find another residence? Thinking about where she would live in a couple of years meant she was projecting. She hadn't even begun working, and now she was planning her future once her tenure with the restoration ended.

Opening a drawer under the countertop, she took out a bibbed apron and slipped it over her dress. The rice was done and so were the beans, and she'd placed them in the warming drawer. Meanwhile the timer on the oven indicated the chicken needed another twenty-five minutes before she could remove it and allow it to rest before carving. She retrieved the platter with a variety of cheese and fruit from the lower shelf of the fridge and set it on the breakfast bar.

"Wow! It's like a work of art."

Sonja's head popped up as Taylor returned to the kitchen. "One can do wonders with cookie cutters." She'd cut strawberries, cantaloupe and honeydew into stars, balls and triangles, and cheese into balls and cubes, alternating each and placing them around a small cluster of white, red and black seed-less grapes.

Taylor moved closer to her. "They look too pretty to eat."

"Pretty or not, we have to eat them or they're going to spoil."

"Have you taken a picture of it?" Taylor asked.

She laughed softly. "No. I have no desire to be-come a food blogger."

"Well, you should start, because once I concoct my dishes I'm going to upload them to your phone."

Sonja gave him a sidelong glance. "I thought we weren't going to compete."

"It's not a real competition. I just want to keep track of the dishes because I don't repeat one too often."

"If it's not real, then it must be fake. Real or not, wannabe Wolfgang Puck, it's on. I just want to warn you that I come from a long line of incredible cooks, and when my dishes beat yours I don't want to see any tears."

Taylor cradled her face. "I never figured you for a trash talker."

Sonja felt his breath feather over her cheek, his mouth mere inches from hers. She'd been totally un-prepared the day before when he'd kissed her. It had happened so quickly that she did not have time to react. "What are you doing, Taylor?" Her query was a whisper.

"Something I shouldn't be doing."

"And what's that?" Her voice had dropped an octave.

A hint of a smile tilted the corners of his mouth. "Deciding whether I should kiss you. If I do, then that negates our promise to be friends."

"And if you don't?"

"Then I will spend the rest of my life wondering how you taste."

Sonja lips parted in a mysterious smile. "How long do you expect to live, Taylor Edward Williamson?"

His smile did not slip as his eyebrows lifted slightly. "Probably ninety-five or maybe even one hundred."

Going on tiptoe, she brushed her mouth over Taylor's. "I'm not going to let you wait—" Her words were cut off in midsentence when Taylor deepened the kiss, caressing her lips until they parted under his. "How do I taste?" Sonja whispered.

Taylor groaned deep in his throat. "Yummy."

"Just yummy?"

"Nah, sweetness. Delicious."

Resting her palms against Taylor's chest, Sonja eased back, breaking off the kiss. Taylor said if he kissed her, then their promise to remain friends would no longer be valid, but what he hadn't known was that she wanted more than friendship. Although she'd vowed, once her divorce was final, that she would never become involved with a man with whom she would work closely, Sonja was no longer a vul-

nerable starry-eyed coed who had succumbed to her
erudite professor. She wasn't that twenty-year-old
wooed by a much older man and married to him at
twenty-one. What she hadn't known after their living together for four years was that she would have
to plan her escape, and then wait another two years
of court appearances with escalating legal fees for
her to obtain her freedom.

That was then and this was now. She'd achieved
her career goal and was now a part of a team responsible for restoring a historic house she predicted
would be written about and photographed for architectural and travel magazines. Her becoming involved with Taylor would be very different from her
involvement with Hugh, because she was ready for a
mature relationship where they could relate to each
other on equal footing. And she had no intention of
marrying Taylor, because their relationship had an
expiration date. Two years.

"You're going to have to let me go so I can check
on the chicken." Although her voice was steady, normal, it wasn't the same with her heart rate. It was
beating so hard and fast she could feel it against
her ribs.

Taylor pressed a kiss to her forehead before releas-
ing her face. Sonja exhaled an inaudible sigh as she
walked to the oven and opened the door. The roaster
had turned golden brown. She inserted a digital thermometer into the thigh to monitor the bird's internal
temperature. To allow the skin to crisp, she had peri-

odically basted the bird in its own juices during the roasting process until it was close to doneness. The thermometer registered 170 degrees. Sonja added another twenty minutes to the timer. The temperature needed to read 180.

She turned to find Taylor staring at her. "It's going to be a while before the chicken is done."

Taylor nodded. "That will give us time to eat what looks like a still-life prop."

Sonja agreed with him. She'd arranged the platter to resemble objects for still-life painters. She motioned to the stools at the breakfast bar. "Please sit. I'll get some plates and forks."

Chapter Nine

Taylor's forefinger traced the stem of his wineglass as he stared across the table at Sonja. Sharing dinner with her had exceeded his expectations.

He had always been very selective when it came to dating. He knew it stemmed from not knowing the identity of his biological father and feared he could possibly be dating his biological half sister. He was certain he and Sonja did not share DNA because of her father's military career. She'd said she was born in a hospital near an army installation on the Kentucky-Tennessee border, whereas the year before, his mother had given birth to him in a Newark, New Jersey, municipal hospital.

Taylor did not have what he thought of as a type

when it came to a woman. He didn't judge them by their appearance, but rather their intelligence and ability to hold his attention, and it was a plus if they shared the same interests.

Picking up the wineglass, he took a sip. "I think you missed your true calling," he said as he smiled over the rim at Sonja.

"And what is that?"

"You should've become a chef. Everything was delicious, beginning with the cheese and fruit, and the rice, beans, and chicken were comparable to what I've eaten at La Casa Del Mofongo."

Sonja shook her head. "I like to cook, but not enough to spend hours on my feet cooking for a lot of people. Been there, done that."

Taylor sat straight. "When?"

"Viola didn't tell you?"

"Tell me what?"

"That I'd been married."

He blinked slowly. Although Sonja had said she didn't have a husband or boyfriend, she hadn't mentioned an ex-husband. "My sister and I don't discuss you."

Sonja gave him a long stare. "I was married while still in college. He—"

"You don't have to tell me about it if you don't want," Taylor said, interrupting her.

"But I do, Taylor," Sonja said in a quiet voice. If she hoped to have a normal relationship with Taylor, then he needed to know some of what she'd gone through with her ex. "I was twenty when I enrolled in an advanced art history class and got involved with my much older instructor. When I agreed to marry him, I had no idea I would become the quintessential trophy wife. I dropped out eighteen credits shy of earning my degree in order to become the hostess for his friends and colleagues."

"How long were you married?"

"We lived together for four years. Once I felt I was being smothered I knew I had to get out, so I waited until he was scheduled to lecture at an exhibition in Denver and left."

"Where did you go?" Taylor asked.

"I stayed with my parents at their retirement home in the Adirondack Mountains and sued Hugh for divorce. He countersued me for abandonment, and I was forced to commute between New York and Boston for court hearings. More than half the time they were postponed when Hugh's attorney wouldn't show up or he would have his doctor claim he was unable to appear because of a medical emergency. This went on for two years until he met someone else and decided it was time to let me go. Meanwhile, I'd moved downstate to live with my aunt and uncle. I enrolled at Pratt and finally got my degrees. End of chapter."

Taylor pushed to his feet, rounded the table, pulled a chair close to Sonja's and draped an arm over her shoulders. "It's the end of that chapter and now a beginning of another, sweetheart."

Sonja rested her forehead against Taylor's. "I

should've said 'end of story' because that's a scenario in my past I don't intend to repeat."

"Are you talking about marriage, Sonja?"

"Yes." The single word was flat, emotionless.

Taylor kissed her curls. "Not all men are like your ex."

"I know that, Taylor. I just don't want to marry again."

"What do you want, *muñeca*?"

Sonja knew this was her opening to talk to Taylor about several ideas she'd thought of for Bainbridge House. "Do you remember when I talked to you about establishing a farm on the property?"

He laughed softly. "How can I forget. You did promise to put everything down on paper."

"I did before I decided to scrap it."

"Talk to me, sweetheart."

Sonja turned her head slightly so Taylor wouldn't see her grin of supreme satisfaction. His fingers gently stroked the nape of her neck as if she were a purring cat, and the gentleness in his voice indicated he could possibly be receptive to hearing her out. "Have you ever eaten at a restaurant with farm-to-table service?"

"No, I haven't."

"If you had, then you'd know what I'm proposing. I haven't looked at the blueprints of the property, but with more than three hundred acres it wouldn't take that much for you to erect greenhouses to produce fruits and vegetables year-round. The dining menu could change with the availability of whatever is in season. There's nothing tastier than freshly picked herbs and greens to accompany a meat, fish or chicken entrée. Sorrel in a salad adds an intense lemony tang. Once you eat a fresh jicama slaw with mango, cilantro and lime you'll want to order it over and over."

Taylor's fingers stilled. "What about chickens?"

This time Sonja did flash a smile for Taylor to see. "There is a distinct difference in eating an egg laid by a chicken earlier that morning and one in a supermarket refrigerated case."

"What happens to the chickens once they stop laying?"

"You kill and eat them, Taylor."

A beat passed. "When I asked my mother about Dad growing up at Bainbridge House, he'd told her they had sheep and ducks on the property."

Shifting slightly on her chair to face Taylor, Sonja met his eyes. "Didn't you say something disparaging about Old MacDonald's farm?"

"Did I really?"

"Yeah. And you know you did."

Wrapping both arms around her shoulders, Taylor pulled her closer. "I'm going to talk to my brother Tariq about your proposal. He's the vet, and he'll be responsible for taking care of any and all of the animals on the property."

"What about the vegetables?"

"After Joaquin restores the garden he'll have to confer with a farmer about where to set up the greenhouses. I can't promise you my brothers will go along with what you propose, but I will do my best to try and convince them."

"I suggest you also talk to Viola about creating a farm-to-table setup. It works so well when held outdoors under a white tent—of course, weather permitting—with long tables and benches, strings of overhead lights, lanterns with flickering votives and music. Depending on the number of guests in any group, you can offer them an alfresco luncheon or dining under the stars."

"That's really casual dining."

"Casual and very chic," Sonja confirmed. "I've toured Italy and France, where I was able to experience farm-to-table dining. During one of my visits to Brittany, I'd checked into a château where I witnessed a late afternoon formal outdoor wedding reception. The groom wore a black wedding morning coat, with a cobalt blue ascot and vest, dove-gray top hat and matching gloves, while the bride was an ethereal vision in Chantilly lace. It was a fairy-tale fantasy in living color."

"Did you take any pictures?"

"Of course I did. Whenever I go abroad I usually have at least three memory cards because I take so many photos."

"What do you do with them?" Taylor questioned.

"I print out the ones I like and then frame them.

Someday, when I buy a house, I plan to transform one of the rooms into an art gallery."

Grinning like a Cheshire cat, Taylor winked at her. "Do you intend to have an exhibition and sell your photos?"

"You got jokes, T.E. Wills?" she asked teasingly.

His grin vanished quickly. "No. And please don't call me that."

"Was your modeling career so traumatic that you want to erase it from your past?"

Taylor dropped his arms and eased back, putting some separation between them. "It wasn't traumatic. In fact, it was very exciting and extremely profitable. I'd rather not talk about that time in my life because it is a reminder of how narcissistic I'd become. For me it wasn't so much about the money as it was which product would give me the highest visibility. After a couple of years, if I had to describe myself, then it would be jaded. I hated going to photoshoots, fittings and fashion shows where I'd have to change in and out of up to ten outfits within minutes. I knew it was time for me to quit the business when someone touched me inappropriately and I went ballistic. Once I calmed down I apologized, but it was too late because behind the scenes I was labeled difficult to work with."

Sonja rested her hand atop his fisted one. "Did you ever think maybe you were experiencing burnout?"

"I knew I was, but I'd become so ego driven that

I feared stopping. I didn't want people to forget or brand me as a has-been. Then, there was my mother constantly asking when I intended to go back to college. I kept telling her one more year and after a while she stopped bringing up the topic. My parents couldn't use the threat of not paying my tuition if I didn't give in to their demands because I was earning enough in one month to cover a year's tuition including books and room and board."

"What did you do with your earnings?"

"I gave them to my father to invest. Dad headed an investment and private equity firm. He had a sixth sense when it came to investing, which made many of his clients extremely wealthy. Dad had instituted a tier system for his clients. The lowest tier was for blue-collar workers who wanted to play the market but didn't have a lot of money to invest. The middle tier was for middle-income professionals, and the top tier was for wealthier clients. He'd assign his clients to designated teams to concentrate on moving those in the lower tier to the middle and the middle to the top."

Sonja was intrigued by Taylor's late father's business model. "Did it work?"

"Yes, it did. His clients had dubbed him the miracle worker, though he was anything but. Dad always said he did not want to take someone's savings and squander it. When the news broke about Bernie Madoff's Ponzi scheme, I saw another side of my father when he talked about hiring a hit man to break every bone in Madoff's body. This pronouncement shocked everyone because we had never witnessed Conrad losing his temper or raising his voice even when he was angry."

Sonja had given Taylor a brief overview about her failed marriage, and now she wanted to know about him aside from his modeling career. "How was it growing up with three brothers?"

Taylor unclenched his fist. "It was a lot of fun, considering we spent so much time together. What's really surprising is we're not competitive with one another."

"Who's the oldest?"

"I am. Patrick is thirty-four, Joaquin thirty-three, Tariq is thirty, and Viola is twenty-eight."

Sonja gave him an incredulous stare. "Your mother had three children a year apart?"

Throwing back his head, Taylor laughed with abandon. "What can I say? When she and Dad bought the house, Mom said she wanted as many children as they had bedrooms. Once she had Viola she claimed her life was complete because she finally had a daughter. Viola upset the equation because it was no longer two against two whenever we formed teams, and we had to figure out a way to include her. To say she was spoiled is an understatement. Mom spoiled her. Dad overindulged her, and she looked to me to protect her against her other brothers whenever they played tricks on her."

Sonja smiled. "There must have been a lot of activity in your home."

"It was whenever we didn't have classes. Mom had transformed her library into a one-room schoolhouse and because we were so close in age, excluding Tariq and Viola, we were given the same instruction."

"Why did you choose to become an engineer?"

"By the time I was ten I knew I wanted to build things because I was obsessed with Lego. I had a table in the corner of my bedroom where I'd created an entire town, and then it was a city with bridges and tall skyscrapers."

"How did your brothers choose their careers?"

"Patrick is a math prodigy. He spent more time at our father's office than any of us. Once he passed the CPA exam he went to work for Dad. We all knew Tariq would become a vet because he took care of our pets. We had dogs, cats, birds, fish, and a family of rabbits that kept multiplying until Mom finally gave them to various pet shops. Joaquin was an enigma because he couldn't decide what he wanted to be until he'd enrolled in college. He'd applied for a part-time position at a local nursery, and that's where his love affair with plants and flowers began. He also fell in love with the nursery owner's daughter and married her."

"Are they still married?"

Taylor shook his head. "No. They were married less than two years and even when pressured Joaquin refuses to discuss the reason behind their breakup. As a landscape architect he has a number of celebrities as his clients."

"Will he also refurbish the golf course?"

The seconds ticked while Taylor appeared deep in thought. "I don't know. That's something I'll have to discuss with Patrick and Joaquin. We have to determine whether having a nine-hole course would be advantageous to guests looking to play several rounds of golf. Perhaps if it could be expanded to eighteen holes, then it could possibly be used as a golf club or for local tournaments."

"What services do you plan to offer your hotel guests?"

"Bainbridge House will become a full-service luxury hotel with restaurants, lounge facilities, meetings rooms, bell and room service."

"What about specialty shops, Taylor? And I'm not taking about the standard gift shop."

Taylor affected a mysterious smile. "What ideas are you hatching in that beautiful head of yours?"

Sonja blushed when Taylor called her beautiful. As the daughter of a black father and Puerto Rican mother she had always thought of herself as an attractive woman of color, but not what she would deem beautiful. "Most luxury hotels have upscale jewelry stores, spas and boutiques. And because Bainbridge House is listed on the National Register of Historic Places you could have an on-site museum shop."

"And what would we sell at the museum shop?"

Her eyebrows lifted. "Do you mean you, Taylor?"

"No, Sonja. I mean *we. If* we do open a museum shop, will you assume the responsibility of running it?"

Her pulse kicked into a higher gear when she thought of the possibility of managing what would become an art gallery. "Yes. If that's what you want?"

"You're the one making the suggestion."

Sonja chose her words carefully. "After I catalogue everything, I'd confer with you about what you'd want to exhibit for sale. Wealthy families during the Gilded Age always purchased duplicate sets of china, silver and crystal for their over-the-top banquets with hundreds of guests. You'll be able to use some of the sets for weddings and retirement dinners, although I recommend purchasing commercial dinnerware, preferably stamped with BH for the restaurants and lounges."

"I can't believe you've planned all of this out even before you begin going through the crates."

Sonja wanted to remind Taylor that she was an art historian and that she'd been involved in countless estate sales. "This is not my first rodeo, Taylor."

"That's obvious." He held up his hands in a gesture of surrender. "I give up, Ms. Rios-Martin. You are hereby responsible for every glass, dish, knife, fork, spoon, table, chair, lamp and rug on the property. And there's no need to confer with me about anything you believe you can resolve on your own."

"Does this mean you're going to consider opening a museum shop?"

"I can't commit to anything until I meet with an architectural engineer. We'll have to reconfigure the entire layout of the first story."

Sonja wanted to remind Taylor there were endless possibilities when renovating an 86,000-square-foot private residence into a hotel and catering venue. While he'd estimated it would take a minimum of two years to completely restore and renovate the mansion and the outbuildings, she had her own timetable for examining, cataloguing and authenticating thousands of items.

"How many hotels have you put up?"

Taylor lifted his shoulders. "I've been involved with a few."

Sonja stared at him as if he'd suddenly grown a pair of horns. "A few! I can't believe you let me go on and on about what goes into a hotel other than rooms—"

"Enough, sweetheart," Taylor said, cutting her off. "I didn't stop you because I wanted to know what you were thinking. I've warmed to your idea of a farm-to-table setup and opening a museum shop on the premises. How many guests can say that they've stayed in a historic hotel and had the option of purchasing an original item that once belonged to the owners."

"I suppose not too many."

"You suppose?"

"All right," Sonja conceded. "Hardly any."

She had visited enough museums and their shops to occasionally purchase a replica of a particular item she just had to have. She had duplicates of Michelangelo's *Pietà* and the *Head of David* in various sizes, and framed reproductions of countless Renaissance Dutch and Spanish painters. Sonja also had begun collecting the work of African American artists from colonial to modern times.

Purchasing her own home had become a priority for both her independence and the ability to display the pieces she'd begun collecting following her divorce. Whenever she purchased a painting, print or sculpture she would have it shipped to her parents' home for safekeeping, with a promise that one day she would come and take her treasure trove to her own home.

"Thank you, Taylor."

"For what?"

"For indulging me."

He gave her a direct stare. "It's not an indulgence, Sonja. I'm open to whatever you have to say."

"Thank you," she repeated.

Sonja did not want to compare Taylor to Hugh. Her ex rarely listened to anything she had to say. The exception was when it benefitted him. Otherwise, he tended to wave her away as if she were an annoying insect. Now that she looked back she wondered how she had surrendered her will to him, and she didn't need sessions with a therapist for the answer. She'd taken her marriage vows seriously while loving Hugh Davies unconditionally.

"Are you ready for coffee and dessert?"

Taylor pressed a kiss to her cheek. "Yes. I'll clear the table while you brew the coffee."

Sonja walked into the kitchen, grinning from ear to ear as a silent voice said Taylor Williamson was a keeper. He was who she needed to start over with—a man who respected her and treated her as his equal.

"I made enough for leftovers," she said over her shoulder. "Should I put away some for you?"

"Of course. What time is dinner tomorrow?"

Sonja went still and then slowly turned to face Taylor. "You want us to eat together every night?"

"That's up to you, Sonja. It can be every night or every other night. The choice is yours."

"Tomorrow is okay. At that time, we can come up with a schedule that works for both of us. If I'm going to make my own hours, then there may be times when I'll work through dinner."

Taylor set stacked plates on the countertop. "Don't…"

"Don't what?" she asked when his words trailed off.

"Just don't overtire yourself."

"I won't. How do you take your coffee?"

"Black."

"Okay. One black coffee coming up."

* * *

Sonja stood at the door watching Taylor as he backed out of the driveway. She waved to him and he returned her wave before she closed and locked the door. Sharing dinner with him was not only enjoyable but also enlightening. After coffee and dessert, he'd stayed behind to help put away leftovers and clean up the kitchen. He'd scraped and rinsed dishes and pots for her to load the dishwasher. How different it was when she'd been left to clean up everything following a dinner party for Hugh's friends and colleagues.

She knew she had to stop comparing Hugh and Taylor, yet the differences were so acute it would take her time—a lot of time—to erase the memories of what she'd had with her ex-husband. When she'd answered Viola's call on Easter Sunday asking whether she would meet her brother, Sonja had no way of knowing her decision would change her life. Turning on her heel, she headed for the staircase. Although curious to open the trunks to see what she would find, Sonja decided to wait until tomorrow.

Chapter Ten

Sonja woke early, showered, slipped into a pair of sweats, and fortified herself with a breakfast of grits, scrambled eggs, crispy bacon, wheat toast and coffee. Then she sat on the floor of the office, opened one trunk and found copies of the floor plans and blueprints Taylor had made for her. She set them aside and began removing bundled letters, receipts, ledgers, and bank and tax records. It was going to take her an inordinate amount of time to put everything in chronological order.

She picked up an envelope with the initials MS—Happy Birthday written on the front in calligraphy. She removed an invoice stamped Paid and a handwritten date of September 4, 1906, for a diamond-

and-emerald necklace from Tiffany's. Sonja jotted the initials, date, item, vendor and the price of the gift on a legal pad. There were more invoices from various jewelry stores in New York, Boston, San Francisco and Philadelphia for MS with dates ranging from 1906 to 1914. The baubles included rings, earrings, multiple strands of cultured and South Seas pearls, totaling more than ninety thousand dollars, which would be the equivalent of more than two million today. Sonja was anxious to determine the identity of MS, who had paid for the jewels, and their connection.

She selected another envelope and spilled out its contents to find ticket stubs and newspaper clippings. Sonja quickly scanned the articles. They were about infamous 1920s gangsters: Bonnie and Clyde, John Dillinger, Charles Arthur "Pretty Boy" Floyd and George "Baby Face" Nelson, just to name a few. There were even more *about* the exploits of Al Capone.

Sonja found herself engrossed in articles about Harry Houdini's death in Detroit, women's official right to vote in the United States, Babe Ruth setting a new home run record, and Lindbergh's first solo flight across the Atlantic. She heard a buzzing and then realized she'd left her phone on vibrate. Scrambling off the floor, she picked the phone off the table. It was her mother.

"*Hola*, Mami."

"*Hola*. How are you?"

Sonja smiled. "I'm okay. No. I take that back. I'm very, very well."

"That's good. I got your text with your new address. I thought you were moving into a hotel."

She flopped down on the blue-and-white-checkered upholstered chair and rested bare feet on the ottoman. "That's what I thought, but my when boss couldn't find one close enough to the work site he rented the condo."

"He sounds like a very generous boss."

Sonja detected a hint of facetiousness in her mother's tone. "He's a very considerate boss, Mami. He needs my expertise, therefore, he's willing to do what has to be done for me to perform at my best."

"Is he married?"

"No."

"Is he engaged?"

Now Sonja was becoming annoyed with her mother's questioning. "I don't think so." She knew Taylor wasn't married, otherwise Olivia would've mentioned it to her. And it was the same with him being engaged. "Why are you asking these questions, Mami?"

"I'm asking because I don't want you to get in and over your head when it comes to him."

Sonja frowned. "Why would you say that?"

"Remember you went gaga over Hugh. When I asked about you spending so much time with him, I recall you saying that he was a helpful and very considerate professor."

Closing her eyes and biting her lip, Sonja struggled to control her temper. She didn't think her mother would bring that up when she'd promised they'd never discuss her ex again once the divorce was finalized.

"Taylor is nothing like Hugh."

"How did you meet him?"

"He's my friend's brother." She told Maria about the phone call between her and Viola, and her subsequently meeting Taylor. "Working at the gallery allowed me to save money, but I knew it really wasn't going to advance my career. But, becoming the architectural historian to restore a residence listed on the National Register of Historic Places was an offer I couldn't refuse."

"I'm not doubting your professional ability. It's just—"

"It's just that you doubt my ability not to mix business with pleasure," Sonja said, interrupting her mother.

Well, she wanted to tell Maria that it was too late. She was doing exactly that, yet there was a difference. She was no longer that twenty-year-old woman who had fallen victim to a much older man who had a habit of preying on his young female students. It wasn't until much later in their relationship that Sonja became aware of his reputation. And when she confronted him, he'd proposed marriage. Shocked and taken aback that he loved her enough to make her his wife, she rationalized the rumors were nothing more than lies and agreed to become Mrs. Hugh Davies.

"I'm not as naive or gullible as I used to be. And I have Hugh to thank for that."

"I'm not trying to run your life, baby. It's just that I don't ever want you to go through what you did with that monster."

"I know that. I told you before that if or when I get involved with someone I'm like a traffic light. Green means go, yellow is proceed with caution and red means stop and don't look back."

"I'm going to ask you one more thing about your boss, and then I promise to stay quiet."

"What's that?"

"Is he nice looking?"

Sonja covered her face with her free hand and inhaled deeply. "No, Mami. He's gorgeous."

Her mother's soft chuckle came through the earpiece. "I rest my case. I never thought when I used to drag you around with me to museums that you would become an architectural historian."

"I love history and I love art even more."

"What are you working on?"

Sonja told her mother about Bainbridge House. "I'm certain if you were to see it restored with the original furnishings you would love it."

"Are you saying they're going to modernize it?"

"No. The exception will be updating the plumbing and electricity. Once the restoration is complete it will look like a French nobleman's country estate.

I'll send you photos when some of the work has been completed."

There was a noticeable pause on the other end of the connection. "When are you coming up to see me?"

Sonja grimaced. She usually tried to visit her parents for a weekend every two to three months, but that was when she worked part-time. "I'm not sure now that I'm working full-time. I don't plan to work the Memorial Day weekend, so I'll probably drive up then."

"We're not going to be here that weekend. Your father and I are driving down to Savannah. He's meeting up with some of his army buddies who rented a boat to sail down to the Caribbean."

"How long will you be gone?"

"About ten days. They plan to use the boat as a hotel while they visit different islands."

"That sounds like fun."

"I'm really looking forward it. I told your father if he agrees to another golf outing that I was going to leave him."

Sonja wanted to tell her mother that she'd threatened to leave her husband so many times over minutiae that James Martin tended to ignore her. "I suppose the next holiday is the Fourth of July. Do you guys also have plans for that holiday weekend?"

"James was talking about surprising me with something because that's our anniversary week, so right now I can't commit to anything."

"I can't believe you're going to be married forty years."

"It doesn't feel like it's been that long," Maria admitted. "I also know you're fixated on your career but—"

"Please don't say it, Mami." Sonja had cut her mother off in midsentence. "I know you want me to find someone and settle down and give you more grandbabies. Of course, I'd like to fall in love and perhaps even marry, but that is not at the top of my wish list. If or when I decide I want to become a mother, I'll adopt."

"I just want you happy, Sonja."

"But I am happy, Mami. I have my health. Right now, I'm living in a beautiful condo where all my needs are met. And I'm working on the sort of project I've always wanted. The only analogy I can think of is an archaeological dig and discovering ancient artifacts."

"I don't want you to think I'm meddling in your life. It's just that I saw you so emotionally wounded that as your mother I, too, felt your pain."

"I've healed and I've never been happier."

"That's what I want to know, baby."

Sonja knew she had pacified her mother because she'd called her baby. "Yolanda told me you sent her your *pastelón* recipe and I got it from her."

"That's because every time I talk to her she nags me until I couldn't stand it anymore and I sent it to her."

"Well, now I have it. I know Abuela is smiling in heaven because her granddaughter will continue the tradition of making her incredibly delicious *pastelón*."

"When we hang up, I'm going to go through some of the recipes my mother left me and send them to you."

"Have you ever thought about writing a cookbook using Abuela's recipes? You could publish it in English and Spanish. You can call it memories of a Puerto Rican kitchen. Before each recipe you can include a little narrative about the events that made that dish so memorable. I remember you telling me how the entire family had to pitch in when making *pasteles* for Christmas." The first time Sonja tasted the tamales filled with pork, chickpeas, yucca, olives, capers and other spices they'd become her personal favorite for the holiday season and other family celebrations.

"Ay dios mío," Maria said, lapsing into Spanish. "Why didn't I think of that?"

"Yo no sé," Sonja answered. It wasn't often she got to speak Spanish, because her mother and uncle, like a lot of New York Puerto Ricans tended to combine the two languages when speaking.

"I'm going to get all of her notebooks and go through them. After I decide what to include, then I'll start writing the narratives. Thank you, baby, for giving me something to do other than sit on the porch and read or watch television."

"Let me know what you come up with."

"I will. I'm going to let you go because I know you have work to do. You can call me whenever you have some spare time."

"Will do, Mami. Love you."

"I love you, too."

Sonja ended the call, smiling. Placing the phone on the charger, she returned to the floor to examine the ticket stubs spanning decades. There had to be hundreds of them from operas, concerts, stage plays, state fairs, circuses, movie theaters, museums and auctions.

Sonja decided the clippings and stubs would take up too much time to catalogue at this time and put them back into the envelope. A collection of flyers garnered her rapt attention. Someone had crossed the Atlantic on a steamship to attend six world's fairs, had taken the train across the country to attend two in San Francisco, driven to Philadelphia and had chartered a yacht to Havana, Cuba. She put them in chronological order. The first was in 1881 to Paris, France, for the International Exposition of Electricity and the last in San Francisco in 1915 for the Panama-Pacific International Exposition's Palace of Fine Arts. She noticed three of the expositions were geared to electricity, and she wondered if the Bainbridges had an interest in Edison's electric lighting system and subsequently invested in General Electric. The trip in 1881 preceded the completion of the château by two years. Where, she wondered, had the

Bainbridges lived before that time? And where and how had they amassed a fortune of at least ten million to build their castle?

Taylor's head popped up when he realized he wasn't alone. The caretaker had entered the room he'd set up to conduct interviews. Earlier that morning he'd met with two licensed electricians and one plumber, and based on their prior experience he wouldn't hire any of them.

"I just closed the gate," the caretaker announced.

Taylor pointed to the chair on the opposite side of the table. "Thanks. Please sit down, Dom." When Elise had talked about a resident caretaker he'd imagined a middle-aged or elderly man living in one of the cottages, not the tall, slender man in his mid-thirties with a black, lightly streaked gray man bun and dark green eyes in a deeply tanned face.

Dominic Shaw sat, stretched out his legs and crossed his booted feet at the ankles. "How did it go?"

Taylor laced his fingers together atop the table. He liked Dom and had come to rely on him to be available when the applicants arrived for their scheduled interviews. He met them at the entrance to the property and escorted them to the main house.

"Although licensed, they are not what I need."

"Not enough experience, Taylor?"

"It's not that, Dom. One electrician admitted that he couldn't get along with his last two supervisors, and for me that is a red flag for someone with a problem accepting and following orders. The other one once had his license suspended. It was recently reinstated, but I didn't want to know why. To be truthful, I'm on the fence with the plumber. He's young, licensed and hasn't had much experience, but I may be able to hire him as an assistant."

"Do you intend to supervise them?"

"Not directly. I'm hoping to hire someone I've worked with in the past to assist me."

"How many general contractors do you need?"

Taylor angled his head. "Why? Do you have someone in mind?"

A hint of a smile parted the caretaker's lips. "Yes."

"Who?"

"Me."

"You?" Taylor repeated.

Dom's smile vanished. "Yes. I'm the fifth generation Shaw caretaker. I learned the ins and outs of repairs from my father and grandfather. They taught me everything about installing electrical wiring and plumbing. By the way, I happen to be a licensed plumber."

Taylor knew the estate's caretakers were paid from a trust set up by Charles Garland Bainbridge in 1898, and at least one Shaw male from each succeeding generation had accepted and maintained the position, including Dominic Shaw.

"Are you asking to work for me?" Taylor asked him.

"No. I won't work for but *with* you," Dom countered. "Conditions set out in trust prohibit me from working for anyone because my sole responsibility is taking care of the estate."

Suddenly Taylor was intrigued with the caretaker. This was the first time they'd had more than a cursory exchange with each other, and Dom's offer to help with the repairs was an unexpected and pleasant surprise. "*If* I agree to let you help with the restoration, what do you want to do?" His query appeared to shock Dom, and he sat up straight.

"I really like plumbing. I renovated my kitchen, put in a half bath, and updated the toilet and all the sinks in my cottage. Would you like to see it?"

Pushing back his chair, Taylor stood. "Sure."

He left the main house with Dom and walked to the six two-story cottages situated far enough from one another for privacy. Dom opened the door to one and stepped aside to let him enter. Taylor wiped his booted feet on the thick straw mat and walked in. The spacious foyer with a circular pedestal table afforded easy access to the living room furnishings from another era. Taylor took in the overstuffed sofas and chairs covered with busy prints, rough-hewn side tables and built-in shelves filled with books, model ships, bottles of spirits and fragile stemware. There were framed black-and-white photos of couples and groups of people from other centuries, and Taylor wondered if perhaps they were Dom's relatives. He smiled seeing the billiard table in an area off the living room.

Dom, noting the direction of his gaze, asked, "Do you play?"

Taylor's eyebrows lifted slightly. "Not in a long time." Conrad had set up a pool table in the game room and had taught all his children to play. There was a chalkboard with a tally, and although he was good Taylor could never beat Joaquin, who demonstrated incredible eye-hand coordination.

"I know you're busy, but you're always welcome to come and test your skills."

"Spoken like a true pool shark."

A flush darkened Dom's tanned face. "I've been known to make a few dollars to supplement my meager income."

"Well, if I'm going to play, then it's not going to be for money because I don't like being hustled."

Crossing his arms over his chest, Dom leaned back on the heels of his boots. "I wouldn't mind playing for a bottle of premium scotch to add to my illustrious collection."

Taylor pointed to the bottles lining the shelves. He'd noticed some were premium aged scotch. "You play for bottles?"

Dom nodded. "Not only am I connoisseur of scotch, but that's the only liquor I drink. I have a few bottles that are at least thirty years old."

"That must have cost the loser a pretty penny."

"It did," Dom said proudly. "But I always say if you can't pay, then don't play."

"I didn't say I can't pay," Taylor countered.

"When do you want to play?"

"Since you issued the challenge, you set the date and time, and I'll let you know if I'm available."

"Tonight?"

"It can't be tonight because I have a prior engagement." He had promised to cook for Sonja. "What about tomorrow night? Say, around eight."

Dom nodded and extended his right hand. "Tomorrow it is. Shouldn't we establish the wager beforehand?"

Taylor shook the proffered hand. "I don't think that's necessary. You want a bottle of aged scotch and I want to clean your clock."

Dom's expression shifted from smug to one exhibiting uncertainty. "Are you some kind of clandestine pool hustler?"

Taylor couldn't help laughing. "No. I grew up with three brothers, and although we all managed to get along we also were very competitive. And it's the same with my sister. It has been a while since I've played the game, but I'm warning you that I'm not an easy target. Now, I want to see what you've done to your kitchen and bathroom because I have to leave and get home."

He'd scheduled the interviews for the morning because he needed time to shop for the ingredients for dinner. He'd sent Sonja a text earlier that morning asking if he could prepare dinner at her place. It would save him having to transport hot dishes from his mother's condo to hers, and she'd quickly replied in the affirmative.

Taylor had to admit the changes Dom had made to the kitchen and bathrooms were remarkable. The sage-green kitchen cabinets, recessed lights, natural plank flooring and a granite-topped table mahogany doubling as an island combined the elements of modern and rustic with the stainless steel refrigerator and dishwasher.

He opened the door under the sink, lay on his back and examined the plumbing hookup. Dom had installed a garbage disposal sink. Taylor checked the strainer basket and the rubber gasket preventing leakage between the strainer body and the sink. Dom had also installed a locknut for tightening the joint between the draining circuit and the end piece. He got up and closed the door. He'd seen enough. The pipes for the cold and hot water supply line, spray hose and the shutoff valve had been expertly installed.

Wiping his hands on the front of his jeans, he nodded. "Very nice."

"Do you want to see the bathrooms?"

Taylor shook his head. "That's not necessary. I'd like to know if I hire a supervisory plumber, are you willing to work with him?"

Dom smiled, exhibiting a mouth of straight white teeth. "I'm your man."

Taylor patted his shoulder. "That means I'll have two plumbers." He needed to interview one more with a license and extensive experience. "I'm telling you this in advance—once I have the entire restoration team, I will have an orientation session where everyone will be introduced to their supervisors. And if anyone has a problem, then the supervisor will handle it, and if they can't then either I or my assistant will step in. At no time will I tolerate bullying or intimidation. And anyone caught or reported will be immediately dismissed and escorted off the property."

"I suppose you mean we'll have to work well with one another."

"That's exactly what I'm talking about, Dom. I will not tolerate a hostile work environment because I'm projecting a two-year timeline."

A slight frown marred Dom's smooth forehead. "Isn't that a little long?"

Taylor shook his head. "No. Remember we're not putting up a building, but restoring a structure to look the way it did one hundred forty years ago. All of the guest rooms will be replicas of that period but with modern amenities like heat, running water, air-conditioning and Wi-Fi. It will be the same with the bar and lounges and meeting rooms. It is much easier to gut a structure and renovate it than restoring it to appear the way it did during a particular era."

"What about the cottages, Taylor?"

"The bedrooms, kitchens and bathrooms will still retain some of the charm of a late-nineteenth-century cottage but with updates that will include air-conditioning and Wi-Fi." Taylor still hadn't decided whether to keep or remove the wood-burning stoves that were used, along with fireplaces, to heat the structures.

"When do you expect to begin the restoration?"

Taylor mentally counted off the weeks. It was now the first week in May and he'd projected it would take him at least a month or maybe even six weeks to interview and hire his teams. "Hopefully before the end of June. I'd like to begin work on the exterior before the cold weather sets in." He recalled what Sonja had said about the windows and roof tiles. "But if I can't get the materials I need to replace the windows and roof tiles before the winter, then we'll concentrate on the interior work until next spring."

"That sounds like a plan."

"Thanks again for volunteering to help. I have to leave now, and I'll see you tomorrow night for our game." It would be another two days before he was scheduled to interview an electrician. And Taylor was still waiting for Robbie to return his call with a date and time for when they could get together.

"No problem, Taylor. You have the remote device for the gate, so just let yourself in."

Wiring the gate electronically was advantageous for Taylor and Dom. Before that he had to call the caretaker to ask him to manually open and close the gates. He walked back to where he'd parked his car. He pressed the remote attached to the visor, opening the massive iron gates, and drove over a metal plate that automatically closed them behind him.

Taylor was looking forward to seeing Sonja again. He knew it wasn't possible for them to spend time together every day, but when they did he wanted it to be special. He'd asked himself whether he wanted to sleep with her, and the answer was a resounding yes. Yet their sleeping together wasn't as much a priority as getting to know each other well enough to say whatever came to mind without insults or reprisals. He didn't want their relationship to become a power struggle as it had been with his former girlfriend. She was one of three female lawyers in a firm of more than twenty, and Taylor had had to remind her over and over they were lovers and not competitors.

Taylor headed for a shopping center several miles from Sonja's condo to buy what he needed to make for their dinner. He loved Italian food and had perfected a favorite recipe, hoping Sonja would enjoy it as much as he did.

Chapter Eleven

Sonja took one last look in the mirror before going downstairs to answer the doorbell. Taylor had called to let her know he would be at her place at four, and that had prompted her to jump in the shower and change out of the sweats and into a pair of stretchy black cropped pants and a black-and-white striped boatneck cotton pullover. She'd brushed her hair off her face and secured it in a bun on the top of her head. She'd just stepped off the last stair when the door opened. It was apparent Taylor had decided to let himself in. He gripped large canvas bags in both hands.

She quickly approached him and closed the door, struggling not to let him see her staring lustfully.

He had paired a white golf shirt with a popular logo with a pair of light gray slacks. Whether in casual or formal wear, his tall, perfectly proportioned physique garnered a second and even a third glance. And there were times when she believed he had caught her gawking as she silently admired his dark complexion and sculptured features.

"Let me help you with some of those."

"It's okay. I've got them."

"Okay, superman."

Sonja followed him into the kitchen. "What on earth did you buy?"

Taylor wiggled his eyebrows. "Stuff."

Bracing a hip against the countertop, she met his eyes. "What's for dinner?"

"Italian bread, Caesar salad, baked clams, penne with ground sausage, sangria and hazelnut gelato."

"You are singing my song. I love Italian food."

"I figured that because you've spent so much time in Italy."

"Do you need a sous-chef?" she asked as he set jars of dried spices, plastic bags of green, red and orange bell peppers, garlic, onion, apples, oranges, lemons, peaches and mushrooms.

"No, babe. Just sit and relax. I'll let you know if I need something. By the way, how was your day?"

"Enlightening."

"How so?" Taylor asked as he continued to take items out of the bags.

Sonja rounded the breakfast island and sat on

a stool. It seemed so natural to have a man in her kitchen as Taylor opened the freezer to store the gelato. "I don't know who MS is, but I found receipts indicating she was the recipient of ninety thousand dollars' worth of jewelry between 1906 and 1914."

Taylor whistled. "That's a lot of money to spend on jewelry during that time."

"It would be equivalent to two million today."

"Maybe MS was Charles Bainbridge's wife?"

"Or his mistress."

Taylor turned and stared at her. "Are you certain of that?"

"No, I'm not. I only found one article written about Charles Garland Bainbridge saying that he'd been prevented from building his summer cottage in Newport, Rhode Island, because there were rumors that his wife may have been a mulatto."

"So you haven't uncovered whether MS is his wife?"

Sonja shook her head. "Not yet."

"Maybe she was his daughter."

"I doubt that, Taylor. Daughters usually inherit jewelry from their mothers or grandmothers."

"What else did you find?" Taylor asked.

"There were ten trips to world's fairs between 1881 to 1915. Did you father ever reveal how his family amassed their fortune?"

He paused for several seconds, seemingly in thought. "I do remember him mentioning railroads, steamships, real estate, theaters and electricity."

Sonja gave herself a mental check when she recalled the number of world's fairs someone had attended with a focus on electricity. "That confirms what I found. There were hundreds of stubs for plays, concerts and films, and receipts for cross-country train trips and transatlantic sailing to Europe for the fairs."

"Judging from the amount of paper in the trunks, it looks as if the Bainbridges were hoarders. Nowadays everything can be saved electronically."

"Once I go through every piece of paper I am going to enter the information on spreadsheets and charts to generate a written history of your family's eminent ancestors."

"They may not be so eminent if you uncover something scandalous."

"No family, regardless of their income or status, is ever scandal-free."

"I suppose you are right, sweetheart."

"You suppose, Taylor? I'm certain your family has its share of secrets."

"I'm certain they do, but aren't families entitled to privacy? Or is it incumbent on them to air their dirty linen just for public consumption?"

Sonja was slightly taken aback by his queries and sharp tone, wondering what he was hiding. Did he know more about his ancestors than he was willing to admit? Or, if she did uncover something immoral or reprehensible, would he demand she not include it in her written report. She recalled him telling her about the clause in his modeling contract prohibiting the agency from disclosing anything about his personal life. What, she mused, was he hiding?

"No, it's not," she answered. "I believe everyone is entitled to a modicum of privacy."

"I believe people are entitled to more than a modicum. Public figures or personalities would fall into the category of the exception. I met a young woman from a very wealthy family, but you wouldn't have known it if she hadn't mentioned it. I don't know whether it was because she feared being preyed upon by those asking for a handout or whether she didn't want to become a target for someone seeking to abduct her for ransom. Whatever her reason, I respected her stance."

"I think you misunderstand me, Taylor. I'm not a newshound looking for dirt on your family to sell to a tabloid. Your hotel will become a living museum, and your guests will want to know about the lives of the people who lived in Bainbridge House."

Taylor halted placing the fruit and vegetables in the sink. "Are you asking me for permission to write a book about the Bainbridge family?"

Sonja hadn't thought about writing a book about his family, but now that he'd mentioned it she suddenly warmed to the idea. "Yes. Depending upon how much I can glean from the trunks, it can be a five-by-eight hardcover with a jacket of Bainbridge House and filled with narratives and photographs of the artifacts. And if I can find photographs of family members it would make it even more factual. Of course, you would have to approve everything before it could be published." She held up a hand when he opened his mouth. "The book could be sold in the museum shop."

Reaching for the retractable sink nozzle, Taylor rinsed the fruit and vegetables. "Did anyone ever tell you that you have a gift for gab?"

She flashed a bright smile. "Yes, but only when I believe in something." It was the second time that day that she'd talked to someone about writing a book. First her mother, and now she was attempting to convince Taylor she wanted to write about his family.

"I'm not going to promise anything at this time, but continue your research, and after you write up your findings we'll go over it together. And I'm warning you that before a single word gets into print, my sister and brothers will have the final say. The decision will have to be unanimous because I have no intention of becoming embroiled in a family feud. When my mother told us about Dad leaving us the property, everyone but Viola decided to get directly involved. The rest of us respected her decision without pointing fingers or trying to strong-arm her to change her mind. My parents raised us to be independent, but to always have one another's backs. If Viola decides she doesn't want to become the executive chef for Bainbridge House then I'm not going to hold that against her. She's her own woman and in control of her destiny."

Sonja didn't know why, but she felt as if Taylor had just chastised her for something she hadn't done. She'd merely mentioned the possibility of uncovering something sordid about his family, and he had taken it out of context. In other words, he was protesting prematurely. In that instant she made herself a promise that she would not bring up the subject again.

She slipped off the stool. "I'm going to set the table."

Taylor knew Sonja was upset and realized he was responsible for the change in her mood. He knew she was excited about what she'd found in the trunks, yet he wasn't the one with the final word as to what the public would be allowed to know about Conrad's family. That responsibility lay with Elise Williamson. She was Conrad's widow, and he'd willed her the property that she in turn had given to her children. Scandal or no scandal, Taylor refused to tarnish the reputation of the family of the man who had become his father and protector in every sense of the word.

"Do you have a glass pitcher or a large carafe?" he asked Sonja as she opened a drawer to remove flatware.

"I have a pitcher, but it's plastic."

"That will have to do. I'm going to need it for the sangria."

"Taylor, you're going to have to let me help with

something because as much as I enjoy looking at you I feel so helpless."

A slow smile parted his lips. "I got you beat there, because there are times when I can't take my eyes off you. Viola never told me what you looked like, so the first time I saw you approach my table at The Cellar I couldn't believe you were real. And when I saw men at other tables sneaking glances at you I wanted to tell them they could look, but I was the lucky dude that night. Then when I met you the next day I was shocked by your transformation. That's when I realized that you're a chameleon and I'd never know what to expect because you manage to look different each time we get together. It could be your hair or makeup or even what you choose to wear."

"Are you saying I keep you off balance?"

"Totally."

"Good."

His smile faded. "Why good?"

"That way you won't take me for granted."

"Is that what you think, Sonja?"

Her eyelids fluttered. "I don't know, but I'm hoping you won't."

Taylor dried his hands on a towel, took a step and rested his hands on her shoulders. "I am not your ex-husband or any of the other men in your life, sweetheart. I'm not perfect, but I've never been accused of taking advantage of a woman, and what I don't want is a relationship with you that will become a power struggle. Yes, I have the power to keep you on the project or let you go, but I hope and pray it will never come to that."

"Are you saying we make a good team?"

Lowering his head, he pressed his mouth to her ear. "We make an incredible team."

"In and out of bed?"

Taylor froze. He'd admitted Sonja kept him off balance, and she had done it again. "Before we go any further, you need to tell me what you want from me."

Easing back, Sonja met his eyes. "Whatever you propose I will let you know without question whether I'm willing to accept or reject it."

"You have to know I'm attracted to you."

"It's the same with me," Sonja admitted. "But how attracted are you? Enough to want to sleep with me?"

Taylor knew it was useless to lie. He had known he was physically attracted to Sonja the instant she'd introduced herself. He'd had no idea whether she was married or engaged, despite not wearing any rings. She could've been in a relationship, but that hadn't stopped him fantasizing about her as an incredibly beautiful and intelligent woman.

"Yes. Enough to sleep with you, Sonja Rios-Martin."

"Wow! You must be serious to mention my entire government name."

Taylor laughed despite the seriousness of their conversation. "That's because I am serious." He sobered quickly. "I need to know if you feel the same about me, however, I don't want to put any pressure on—"

"Not to worry," Sonja interrupted. "I will not succumb to pressure from you or any man to sleep with him. You know that I like you, Taylor—a lot. But I must figure out if history is going to repeat itself if I decide to sleep with you. What I didn't tell you was that my ex had been one of my professors. Something told me it was wrong to get involved with him, yet I refused to listen to my inner voice."

Taylor brushed a light kiss over her parted lips. "This time I want you to listen to your inner voice. If it tells you not to sleep with me, then don't do it. And if we do share a bed, then that decision will have to be yours and yours alone."

Sonja wondered why she hadn't met Taylor earlier in her life, when she could've had a relationship with him rather than a man that treated her more like an object than his wife. "You know if I'd met you when I was twenty, my life would've turned out drastically different."

Attractive lines fanned out around Taylor's large dark eyes when he smiled. "I doubt we would've crossed paths because my life revolved around modeling and I had little time to devote to a girlfriend or even have a lasting relationship. And marriage wasn't even on my radar."

"Has it ever been on your radar, Taylor?"

"Only when my mother tells me I'm going to wind

up an angry, lonely old man because I'm too selfish to share my life with a woman."

"Do you agree with her?"

'No. I try and tell her that when the right woman comes along, I'm certain she will be the one I'd want to spend the rest of my life with."

"So, you are open to marriage."

"Of course I am," Taylor said adamantly. "What gave you the impression I wasn't?"

"I don't know. You're thirty-five, unencumbered, and I just thought you were quite satisfied with your status and lifestyle."

"I am unencumbered and comfortable with, as you say, my status and lifestyle, but that doesn't mean I can't change it whenever I choose. What about you, Sonja? Do you think you'll ever remarry?"

It took several seconds for her to say, "I don't know. There were times when I told myself *once burned, twice shy*, and never again. However, lately things in my life have changed."

"How so?"

"This is the first time since leaving home to attend college that I've felt like an independent adult. I had a college roommate, then I married Hugh, and after leaving him I stayed with my parents until my divorce was finalized. Then when I reenrolled in college to get my degree I lived with my aunt and uncle. And I was still living with them until two days ago when I moved here."

"Why did you continue to live with them after you graduated?"

"I was staying with them rent-free because I was saving money to buy a house or condo. But that wasn't happening, because most of my jobs were either as a substitute teacher or part-time."

Taylor smiled again. "Until now."

She returned his smile with a bright one of her own. "Yes. Until now."

"You could buy this condo if you want."

Sonja stared at Taylor as if he had taken leave of his senses. First he told her the units were overpriced, and now he was saying she could buy it. "I suppose I could if I rob a bank," she quipped.

"Even though you look incredible in the color, I don't want to see you wearing an orange jumpsuit."

Sonja landed a soft punch on his chest. "I was just joking."

"And I wasn't joking about you buying this condo. That's something we can discuss once the lease expires."

Sonja was aware that the lease on the condo, her SUV and the credit card Taylor had given her, were all charged to Bainbridge House Trust, Inc., and at the end of her two-year contract she would not only have a history of steady employment, she also would've saved enough money to put down on a house or condo.

"I'm going to get that pitcher for you."

Taylor released her. "If you want you can cut up

the fruit for the sangria while I make the dressing for the salad."

"Do you need an apron?" she asked him. "After all, you are wearing white."

He glanced down at his shirt. "I'll take one as long as it doesn't have ruffles."

Sonja made a sucking sound with her tongue and teeth. "Sexist." Turning on her heel she went to the pantry to get one of several aprons she'd bought. She wore an apron when cooking because it was something her mother said every woman in her family always did whenever they cooked.

"This one is a little large for me, so I double it up and tie it twice around my waist."

Taylor unfolded the apron and smiled when he saw what was printed on the bib. "Kiss the Cook?"

Sonja rolled her eyes upward. "Yeah. It was the only one left, so I was forced to buy it."

He slipped it over his head, secured the ties and beckoned to her. "Come here, babe, and kiss the cook."

She took a step back. "Stop it!"

"Not until you kiss the cook," he crooned.

Sonja rested her hands at her waist. "And if I don't?"

Taylor stalked her like a large cat. "You don't want to know."

Then with a motion too quick for her to follow, she found herself in his arms, her feet several inches above the floor and her mouth covered in a kiss that stole the very breath from her lungs. Her arms went around Taylor's neck to keep her balance, and she found herself kissing him back, her tongue as busy as his as she tried to get even closer. It had been so long, much too long since the passion that lay dormant had flared to life. She heard a deep moan, not realizing it had come from her. She was on fire— everywhere, and Sonja knew Taylor was the only one to extinguish it.

It did not matter that she worked for his family and that her career and the next two years of her life depended on the man with whom she had fallen inexorably in love. Sonja had known Taylor was someone she never should have become involved with once she recognized him as T.E. Willis. Although he had left the world of modeling where he'd become an icon, she'd had second thoughts about working for Taylor Williamson, the engineer.

At first she thought her attraction was because of his gorgeous face and perfect masculine body, and then she chided herself for acting like an adolescent obsessing over her favorite actor or performer. After all, she was a woman in her midthirties who had been married and now was mature enough not to go, as her mother said, gaga over a man who had made a name for himself in his chosen field.

The more time she spent with Taylor the more she liked what he presented. He hadn't come on to her like some men she'd worked with or who had come into the gallery. He was the perfect gentleman that she was certain her mother would approve of. And she'd never had a man ask permission to kiss her. Hugh thought it was his right to kiss her when she wasn't expecting or even ready for the gesture the first time they were alone together at his house. He'd believed because she'd agreed to come to his home that she would agree to anything. She had come close to punching his lights out when he saw her expression and apologized profusely. His apology had been enough for her to agree to see him again, unknowingly to her detriment.

But it was so different with the man holding her to his heart. He respected and treated her as an equal, for which she was grateful. Sonja had lost count of the times she'd told herself that she liked Taylor as a friend, but that inner voice told her she was a liar, that there was nothing friendly about her thoughts. In fact, they bordered on erotic fantasies, and that when she'd told herself she was sex-starved it was because it had been almost ten years since she'd slept with a man.

Taylor had been forthcoming when he admitted he wanted to sleep with her and had given her the option of acting or not acting on it. What he hadn't known was the second time she saw him she'd wanted to jump his bones.

"Taylor."

"What is it?" he whispered against her mouth.

Sonja felt the runaway pumping of his heart against her breasts and knew if he didn't let her go she would shame herself when begging him to take her upstairs and make love to her. "You have to let me go."

"What if I don't want to?" He'd released her mouth and pressed his mouth against the column of her neck.

"You have to, because I'm not ready for this." Her statement must have gotten through to him. He loosened his hold on her body and lowered her until her feet touched the floor.

His eyes appeared abnormally large under the recessed lights as his chest rose and fell heavily as if he'd run a grueling race.

"Do you think you'll ever be ready?"

Sonja knew it was time for honesty if she hoped to have an open and uncomplicated relationship with him. "Yes. Please give me time to get my head and heart together."

Taylor stared at her from under lowered lids. "Take all of the time you need, sweetheart. After all, we have two years to get it right."

"You're right." He was giving her more time than she needed.

"I don't know about you, *muñeca*, but I'm hungry as a horse, so let's get to cooking."

Sonja couldn't believe she had eaten so much. The stuffed clams were the best she'd ever had, and there had been more than a few in her life when there were more bread crumbs than chopped clams. Taylor had cooked bacon until crisp and then crumbled it and set it aside while he sautéed onion, pepper and garlic until tender. He had then combined bread crumbs, oregano, grated parmesan cheese and the sautéed vegetables with the fresh chopped clams he'd gotten from the supermarket's fish department. He filled the shells with the mixture, sprinkled them with parsley and paprika and, after drizzling them with virgin olive oil, placed them in the hot oven until the tops were browned and the mixture bubbly. The Caesar salad with homemade dressing, warm buttered Italian bread and the delicious penne with ground sausage rounded out an incredible dinner, comparable to those served in restaurants.

She dabbed the corners of her mouth after swallowing a mouthful of sangria. "Who in the world taught you how to cook like this?"

"My mama."

Sonja slumped back in her chair. "You're kidding?"

"Nope. My mother made breakfast, lunch and dinner for us Monday through Friday. On the weekends it was either brunch and a light dinner or we went out to restaurants. Brunch was always a family affair with everyone cooking what they wanted to eat. The menu included omelets, waffles, pancakes, bacon, sausage, ham and cheese grits. We had live-in help that cleaned and did laundry, but Mom insisted on cooking for her children. We accused her of being paranoid, afraid someone would poison her kids."

"What did she say?"

"She completely ignored us. Mom had dozens of cookbooks and she planned her meals the same as she did her lesson plans. Each of us was assigned a week to watch and assist her preparing dinner. She was harder on her boys because she claimed she didn't want us hooking up with the wrong woman just because she could cook, and we couldn't."

"I have to assume her cooking lessons were successful because you are an incredible cook."

"Tariq and Patrick are even better than I am. They've mastered Asian and Middle Eastern cuisine. Joaquin and I are about equal, but it's our baby sister who surprised and surpassed everyone. That's why she's a professional chef."

"What about your father?"

"Dad was completely clueless in the kitchen. During the week, he usually got home too late to eat with the family, and that's why he devoted the entire weekend to us. His office was in Manhattan and he was up and out of the house to take the early train into Penn Station. There were nights when he didn't leave the office until late and had a car service on call to bring him home because a few times he'd overslept on the train and missed his stop. His edict to his employees was never to call him at home on weekends. That was his time for his family, and he couldn't be bothered with what he called minutiae that could wait for Monday morning. He'd called it minutiae, but there were a few times he substituted an expletive when he thought we were out of earshot. My parents were very free thinkers and proud to be labeled liberals, and although not ultrareligious, we did attend church services. They would not allow cursing in their home. It wasn't until I went to college that I was given a crash course in cuss words."

Sonja laughed. "I forget you were homeschooled until you left for college. Did you have to wait until then to date?"

"No. Once I got my driver's license, I hung out at the spots where many of the local high school kids gathered. Although many viewed me as an outsider I did manage to make a few friends."

"If you had children, would you consider having them homeschooled?" Sonja asked.

"That would all depend on their mother. My mother was certified to teach grades K through twelve and was also a reading specialist. She'd converted the library into a one-room schoolhouse, and floor-to-ceiling bookshelves were packed with books she'd inherited from her mother and grandmother. During the school year, we rarely watched television or played video games because we spent most of our free time reading or hanging out in the game room putting together thousand-piece puzzles, competing with one another playing pool, Ping-Pong or teaming up for board games. Summers were spent outdoors playing tennis and basketball, and swimming."

Sonja neatly folded her napkin and placed it next to her plate. Again, she envied Taylor and his siblings for their closeness. As the eldest, Taylor was seven years older than his youngest sibling, while her brother was ten years her senior. It wasn't that she and her brother did not love each other. However, it was the difference in their ages that had made it difficult for them to share a lot of the same activities.

"Oh! I forgot to tell you that I went online to look up companies in Italy that manufacture the windows you need to replace the ones in the château. I've also compiled a listing of Vermont quarries for the roof tiles. I'll send both to your email."

"I need to order two hundred forty-two windows. If we're not able to get them from Italy in time to install them before the winter, then they will be replaced with custom-made duplicates. What I will need from you is the name or names of faux bois specialists to restore the walls and moldings."

Sonja nodded and made a mental note to call someone she knew who owned an art restoration service. "I'll try and get that information for you. I'm going to spend one more day going through the trunks before heading over to the house to start with the crates."

"I'll have the caretaker give you a remote device to operate the front gates, and that way you won't have to call him in advance. My Thursday schedule is filled with back-to-back interviews, so I doubt whether I'll get to see you. I'll also make certain some of the crates are brought up from the cellar and into in the library."

"Thank you," she said, and then quickly covered her mouth with her hand to smother a yawn. "Sorry about that. Red wine always makes me sleepy." Even when traveling through Europe she'd made certain not to drink red wine if she'd planned to stay up for any appreciable amount of time.

"Why don't you go into the family room and chill. I'll clean up here."

"You don't have to, Taylor. You cooked, so I'll clean up."

He stood. "Not tonight, babe."

Sonja knew it was useless to debate the issue when Taylor rounded the table and scooped her up in his arms. He carried her into the family and lowered her to the love seat. She smiled up at him when he leaned over her. "I'm just going to rest my eyes for a few minutes."

She had no idea that resting her eyes for a few minutes would translate into falling asleep, and when she awoke she discovered she was in her own bed. Apparently, she had not woken up when Taylor carried her up the staircase. Rising on an elbow, she glanced at the clock on the bedside table. It was after ten. Sonja did not want to believe she'd been asleep for nearly two hours.

She closed her eyes while fantasizing about how much she'd wanted to wake up with Taylor in bed with her. He was everything she wanted in a man, yet old fears would not let her acknowledge what she'd been feeling for a while. She was falling in love with her friend's brother. They'd talked about marriage and children, and perhaps if Hugh had not turned into a monster she would be more receptive to a man's attention. It had taken years for the emotional scars fade, but she did not know if they would ever completely disappear.

Sonja opened her eyes and moaned at the same time she rolled her head on her neck. Her shoulders were achy from sitting on the floor hunched over for hours earlier in the day. She knew it was time to use the table doubling as a desk to do her work. Slipping off the bed, she headed for the bathroom to brush her teeth and wash her face. After changing out of her clothes into a cotton nightgown, she got back into bed and fell asleep for the second time that night.

Chapter Twelve

"I can't believe you came all this way for a pool cue."

Taylor dropped a kiss on his mother's hair when she closed the book she'd been reading and rose from the rocker where she'd sat awaiting his arrival. "Don't get up, Mom."

Elise sat down once Taylor took the rocker opposite her. "You didn't answer my question, Taylor." Her sapphire-blue eyes narrowed. "What's bothering you son?"

Stretching out long legs, Taylor crossed his feet at the ankles and stared at the scuffed toes of his running shoes. He'd made a mental note to throw them away a long time ago but was loath to part with them because one of his pet peeves was trying on shoes. In fact, he didn't like shopping and trying on clothes because of the years he'd spent standing motionless while designers and tailors adjusted an inseam or the length of jacket sleeve. Then there were the fashion shows where, within seconds of leaving the runway, he was stripped of whatever he was wearing for a new outfit while a makeup artist fussed over his face.

"What makes you think something is bothering me?"

"When are you going to accept that I probably know you better than you know yourself, Taylor? Call it a mother's intuition, but I know when my children are happy, angry and troubled. And right now, something is troubling you, and I hope it's because of a woman."

Taylor gave his mother an incredulous stare. Either he was that transparent or she that intuitive. He knew it was useless to lie her because it was something he rarely did. "I did come to get my pool cues."

"Who is she?" Elise asked.

He frowned. "Now I know where Viola gets her tenacity—you're both like dogs fighting over a bone when you think you're onto something."

Elise smiled as a network of fine lines appeared around her eyes. "Well, after all she is my daughter." Her smile faded. "Talk to me, Taylor, about this woman that probably has been keeping you up nights."

"I did meet someone."

"Is she a nice girl?"

Taylor closed his eyes and shook his head. Whenever any of his brothers talked about dating a woman, Elise always asked if she was a nice girl. "Yes, Mom. She's a very, very nice girl." He wanted to tell his mother that Sonja wasn't a girl but a woman.

"Tell me about her."

He told her everything, beginning with Sonja walking into the restaurant to their sharing dinner the night before. He did not tell his mother that he'd wanted to make love to Sonja and would have if she'd given him permission. "She's so different from the other women I've known that it's scary."

"That's because you're in love with her, Taylor. You may have liked the other women you dated, but I'm willing to bet you weren't in love with them."

"I don't know. Maybe I don't know what love is. I know I love you, my sister and my brothers, but that's different from what I feel for Sonja."

Elise rested her head against the back cushion and closed her eyes for several seconds. "I know what you're feeling, son, because I felt the same way when I met your father for the first time. He was one of the best-looking boys on campus. However, it wasn't his looks that made me fall in love with him—it was his charm and sensitivity. Whenever we were together I felt as if I were only woman in the world because he treated me like a princess. It took me a long time to admit I'd fallen in love with him, and once he asked me to marry him I knew I wanted to spend the rest of my life with him. That's what you must ask yourself. Can you see yourself spending the rest of your life with this woman?"

Taylor had asked himself the same question, and the answer was surprisingly yes. "Yes, I can. But what I find so strange is that I really don't know her. I met her for the first time about six weeks ago, and since then I can't get her out of my head."

"You don't want her in your head?" Elise asked.

Taylor wanted to tell Elise that he wanted Sonja in his bed, and then perhaps he'd be able to get her out of his head. When he'd spied her approaching his table, his initial attraction to her had been wholly physical, and that hadn't waned. "I don't know what I want at this point in time."

"Why are you measuring your relationship within segments of time, Taylor? Some couples meet and fall in love at first sight, marry right away and then go on to have a long and happy life together. Others take longer because the timing isn't right. Your father and I dated for two years because we were young and had goals to accomplish. You're exactly where you want to be in your career. You don't have to concern yourself with not having enough money because you were a millionaire even before you celebrated your twenty-fifth birthday. Now, what's holding you back from telling this woman that you love her?"

Taylor realized he wasn't telling mother everything about Sonja. "She was married to a man that was a lot older than she was. I think it scarred her, and she really doesn't trust men."

Elise sat straight. "Had he physically abused her?"

"I don't think so. If there was abuse, then it had to be either emotional or even psychological. In any event, she said she'd felt smothered and had to get out. And whenever we talk about marriage, she claims she never wants to marry again."

"Maybe you can get her to change her mind."

"I don't want to change her mind, Mom. That decision must be hers. And what I refuse to do is shack up with a woman. If we're going to live together, then she has to be my wife."

Elise glared at Taylor. "Sonja is not your mother, Taylor. She made the mistake of living with a man that deserted her when she needed him most. It's different with you and Sonja because you are *not* living together. If you love the woman, then let her know and wait for her to come around. If she does tell you that she loves you, then don't put any pressure on her to marry. That must be her decision."

"Are you saying we should live together?"

"There are worse things in this lifetime." She crossed her arms under her breasts. "Wake up, Taylor. This is not the forties, fifties or even the early sixties, when living together was akin to living in sin." Elise waved a hand. "I can't believe I raised someone with such antiquated views of life."

"I'm not that old-fashioned," Taylor mumbled under his breath.

"Enough talk about your love life, now tell why you want your pool cues."

"I have a little wager with Dom Shaw that I can beat him. And if I lose then I must hand over a bottle of aged scotch. I need to go through Dad's liquor cabinet and find a bottle." Conrad was also a collector of aged brandy, whisky and scotch.

"Take whatever you need because you know I won't touch the stuff."

"Maybe the next time I come I'll box them up, take them to the house and store them in the cellar with the wine."

"If you're shooting pool with Dom, then you'd better be careful."

"Why would you say that?" Taylor asked Elise.

"Because his father was a pool shark, and Conrad said he remembered him conning some of the household help."

"Well, Dad, was no slouch, and I learned from the best."

Elise laughed softly. "You're right about that. I used to accuse him of turning our kids into pool hustlers."

"Thankfully he didn't, and we all turned out all right."

"I suppose I should take some credit for that. How is everything going at the house?"

"Slow, Mom. I've interviewed a few candidates, and right now I'm considering hiring one. I have to see a few more tomorrow and hopefully before the end of the month I will have everyone onboard."

Elise nodded. "What's good is that you've given yourself a realistic timeline in which to complete everything."

Taylor agreed with her. There was nothing worse than pressuring workers to fast-track a construction project, which sometime resulted in on-site accidents and possible violations.

"Do you know where you'll live once the hotel is open for business?"

"I'd like to move into one of the cottages."

"That's a good choice. I was really surprised to find the rooms were much larger than they appeared from the outside. And three bedrooms is perfect for a couple with a one or two children."

"Maybe you can convince Patrick to move back east and live in one with his new bride"

A scowl distorted Elise's normally pleasant visage. "If he moves back, then I prefer he be alone."

Taylor could not understand his mother's disdain for his brother's fiancée. It was true that Andrea was spoiled and used to having her way, but that was Patrick's problem. "No comment."

"You say no comment when you should be the one warning him that he's going to ruin his life if marries that brat."

"I'm not going to interfere with my brother's love life. When he's had enough, he'll do what he must to extricate himself from what you see as a toxic relationship. Meanwhile, I suggest you don't bring it up with him because Patrick will only resent your interference."

"It's amazing how you always take up for him," Elise said angrily.

Taylor didn't want to get into it with his mother about his brother. As the eldest he'd been the one to protect his younger siblings, something he'd felt duty-bound to do even as an adult. Pushing to his feet, he forced a smile. "I'm going inside to get my cues and a bottle of scotch."

Elise reached out and caught his hand. "I'm sorry for what I said about you taking up for Patrick."

Leaning down, he kissed Elise's forehead. "No harm done, Mom. I know you love Patrick and only want the best for him."

"I want the best for all my children."

"We know that." He kissed her again, this time on her cheek.

Taylor left Belleville, his head full of what he'd admitted to his mother about falling in love with a woman who was more a stranger than he'd realized. If anyone had told him he would find himself in love with a woman he was beginning to think of as his counterpart, and, more importantly, a woman with whom he could be himself, he probably would've laughed.

He knew if he told Sonja that he'd fallen in love with her she'd probably believe he was crazy, or she would run in the opposite direction. She would remind him of the fact they were strangers and hadn't known each other long enough to profess an emotion as strong as love. And while he was ready to marry and have children, she wasn't. That had become his reality.

Taylor realized he had it all, but there was something missing. He'd been adopted into a warm, loving family; had found fame and fortune as a top male model; realized his boyhood dream to become an engineer, and now claimed one-fifth of a mansion appraised at 150 million dollars.

Ten minutes into his drive, Sonja's number appeared on the navigation screen. Smiling, Taylor answered the call. "What's up, sleepyhead?" Her sultry laugh came through the speakers.

"Please don't remind me of that. That's the last time I'm going to drink red wine when I'm with you."

"If you do, then there's one thing you'll know."

"And what's that?"

"That I'll never take advantage of you." There came a pause, and Taylor waited a full ten seconds before he said, "Sonja? Are you still there?"

"Yes, I am. And I want to thank you."

"For what?"

"For not taking advantage of me."

It was his turn to pause. Just what did she think he was? Some pervert who would take advantage of a woman under the influence? "I would never do that, especially with you or any other woman."

"Why me, Taylor? Is it because I'm your sister's friend?"

"My sister has nothing to do with what goes on between you and me. I told you before that I wouldn't discuss you with Viola, because she knows not to get into my personal life."

"Point taken."

"Is it, Sonja? Because you keep bringing up Viola."

"Okay, Taylor. I won't bring her up again."

Taylor heard the slight edge in her voice and hoped he hadn't come on too strong. "Look, babe, I'm sorry if you—"

"There's no need for you to apologize, *papi*."

Taylor grinned from ear to ear when he registered the endearment. *"Gracias, muñeca."*

Sonja laughed again. "Look at you speaking Spanish."

"I'm trying, sweetheart. I figure if we're going to hang out together for the next few years I could become fluent."

"How many years of French did you have?"

"Three, maybe four."

"You told me your mother spoke fluent French, yet you don't speak the language."

"I understand and read it better than I can speak it."

"Well, if you want to learn Spanish, then you have to speak it."

"Can I hire you to become my tutor?" he teased.

"I doubt if we're going to spend that much time together once you really get involved in the restoration."

"How about weekends?"

"Weekends are fine, Taylor, if I'm not working."

"No one will work weekends, and that includes you, Sonja."

"Is that an order?"

"No. That's the company policy."

"I thought you told me you're an easygoing boss."

"I am. But there are certain rules that must be followed, and no-work weekends is one of them. Weekends are for families. During the months of July and August, contractors will be given Fridays off. After the Labor Day weekend, they will resume their Monday through Friday schedules."

"Isn't it different for me, Taylor because after all I am a contract worker, and I can make my own hours."

"That's true. But wouldn't you want to spend some time with your parents, or aunt and uncle?"

"I hadn't thought of that."

"Well, I have. I can't have you burned-out before we have our grand opening."

Taylor wanted to tell Sonja it was something he also was looking forward to. He wanted to schedule the grand opening for late spring when the trees and flowers were in bloom, and host a reception in one of the ballrooms for the press, local, state and national politicians.

"That's something I don't intend to miss. Thankfully, that's quite a way off because I estimate it's going to take me a long time to catalogue everything, and especially now that you tell me there's even more crates than the ones I saw."

Taylor chuckled. "Maybe I shouldn't have mentioned that to you."

"I'm glad you did because I don't like surprises, Taylor."

He sobered. "I'll try and remember that." He wondered if Sonja would be surprised or even shocked if he told her he was in love with her.

"I just sent you an email with the information you asked for. The guy that owns the restoration company is a doll. I told him what you needed, and he said he'll get back to me and let me when someone can come out and view the damage. Of course, I'll check with you to see when you're available."

"Thanks, sweetheart."

"I'm going to hang up now because I want to finish what I'm working on. Then I'm going downstairs to heat up some of your delicious leftovers."

"Okay. I'll probably see you tomorrow at the house."

"That's a bet. Later, Taylor."

"Later, love."

Love, he thought. How had the single word slipped out so easily when he had made a concerted effort during their conversation not to tell Sonja that not only had he fallen in love with her?

Taylor drove along the paved path to Dominic Shaw's cottage. His mother's warning that Dom's father had been a pool shark only served to heighten his competitiveness. And if the son was anything like his father, then Taylor wanted to warn the caretaker he didn't intend to be that easily maneuvered into handing over a bottle of aged single malt scotch whisky.

Dom opened the door at the same time Taylor alighted from the SUV. Reaching for the case with the cue sticks, Taylor grasped the velvet bag with the bottle and handed it to Dom. "Careful with the prize."

Dom opened the bag and smiled. "This Balvenie Caribbean Cask 14-year-old single malt whisky will go nicely with my collection."

"Nah, son."

"Who are you calling son? I bet I'm older than you."

"You," Taylor countered, smiling.

"Nah, Taylor. I just celebrated my thirty-fifth birthday."

"I'll be thirty-six in November, so I've got a few months on you." When meeting Dominic for the first time, Taylor realized despite the fact he was graying there wasn't a single line on his face or around the brilliant dark green eyes. Tall and almost rawboned, there wasn't an ounce of fat on his lean body. "What I'm going to do is beat the hell out of you, and then I'm going to crack open that bottle and have a few shots and you're going to join me rather than sit back and admire it on your shelf."

Dom laughed loudly. "You talk a lot of shit, old man. Let's go inside and have a go at it. Better yet, why don't we crack open this baby and sample it while we play?"

Taylor gave him a direct stare. "I thought you wanted to add it to your collection. Could it be that you're afraid I'm going to beat you?"

"Not really. I'm more than confident that I can hold my own, but when I saw that you brought your own cue sticks I realized you're no novice."

"In other words, you realized you couldn't hustle me."

A flush darkened Dom's face under his tan. "I don't hustle folks. I've lost some games and won many more."

"Okay. Let's go inside and find out if you're going to win some and lose many."

Taylor had to admit that Dom just wasn't good. He was an expert. In fact, his eye-hand coordination was comparable to that of Joaquin, who could've turned pro if he hadn't chosen to become a landscape architect.

They played the best of five, and Dom won three and Taylor two. After each game they took a shot of whisky, and Taylor knew he had to stop; otherwise, he wouldn't be able to get behind the wheel and drive. "I'm done."

"Don't you want to play one more?" Dom asked.

"No. What I need to do is sober up before I leave."

"I have two extra bedrooms where you could crash."

"I don't want to impose."

"You won't be imposing, Taylor. After all, you do own this cottage."

"My family owns it," Taylor said, correcting him. "I'm going to sit here for a while."

"I'm going to the kitchen to make some coffee. You're not the only one feeling the effects of the whisky. This is the first time I've tasted The Balvenie. It definitely lives up to its reputation, and drinking it is a lot more enjoyable than staring at the bottle."

"I agree," Taylor drawled. He rarely drank hard liquor, but when he did it was only from his father's bar. The soft and lingering notes of toffee and vanilla with a hint of fruit on his palate made the single malt whisky exceptional.

Dom returned with two mugs of steaming black coffee. He handed one to Taylor. "Drink up, old man. I added a couple of shots of espresso to yours."

Taylor smiled. "Don't push it, son." He took a sip of the hot brew, grimacing when it burned his tongue. Staring at Dom while waiting for his coffee to cool somewhat, he wondered what had made a supposedly healthy thirtysomething-year-old man live alone on an abandoned estate.

"I forgot to ask if you wanted milk in your coffee."

"No, thanks." A beat passed. "Do you like living here?"

Dom stared at Taylor over the rim of his mug. "Yes, because it's all I know. I was born here, and I'll probably die here. The only time I left was when I enlisted in the service and then attended college, but like a homing pigeon I came back."

Taylor knew very little about the caretaker. "What did you study in college?"

"I have a master's in Business."

Taylor was surprised by Dom's revelation. He did not want to believe the man was licensed plumber and had earned a graduate degree yet was content to live on an estate in the role as a glorified maintenance man. It was obvious Dom had his reasons for wanting to live out his life on the Bainbridge property.

He managed to finish the coffee, and the extra caffeine was enough to clear his head and jolt him into alertness. "Thanks for the coffee," he said, pushing off the sofa and coming to his feet.

Dom also stood. "Are you sure you're okay to drive?"

"I'm good."

"Aren't you going to take your cue case?" Dom asked as Taylor walked to the door.

"No. I'm going to leave it here for when we play again."

Dom followed Taylor to the door and opened it. "I'm looking forward to it."

"No shots," Taylor said.

"No shots," Dom repeated, laughing loudly.

Taylor paused. "Oh, before I forget. The architectural historian is coming tomorrow, and I want you to give her one of the remote devices for the front gates. Her name is Sonja Rios-Martin, and she has no set work hours. My schedule is filled with back-to-back interviews, so I doubt I'll get to see her."

"No problem."

Taylor made it home and once he opened the door to his mother's condo he cursed himself for engaging in what he thought of an as asinine frat boys' game. He did not want to believe that he'd waited until thirty-five to do shots.

Never again, he mused. It would be the first and last time, he vowed as he brushed his teeth and rinsed with a peppermint mouthwash. He stripped off his clothes, leaving them in the hamper, and stepped into the shower stall. Ice-cold water rained down on his head and body before Taylor adjusted the temperature to lukewarm.

After drying off, he walked in the direction of the guest bedroom and fell across the bed. His last thoughts before Morpheus claimed him were of Sonja as he stood beside her bed, watching her sleep.

Chapter Thirteen

Decelerating, Sonja turned onto the private road leading to Bainbridge House. Some of the older trees that had been still bare the last time she'd come to the estate were now resplendently covered with bright green leaves. She drove through the open gates and seconds later they automatically closed behind her. She wanted to get to the house by eight and work nonstop until midafternoon. Maneuvering into the driveway behind Taylor's car, she shut off the engine. It was obvious she wasn't the only one planning to begin early.

Scooping up the tote with her camera, legal pads and felt-tipped pens, and the insulated bag with her lunch in glass containers filled with salad, fruit and bottles of water she got out of the SUV. She climbed the six steps, opened the front door and came face-to-face with a tall, slender man dressed entirely in black: shirt, jeans and boots. Sonja forced a smile she didn't quite feel because there was something about him that made her uncomfortable. The dark green eyes the exact shade of peridot had deepened to a dark emerald the longer he stared at her. She wanted to ask him if he'd been taught it was impolite to stare.

"I'm Sonja Rios-Martin," she said, shattering the soporific spell.

The man inclined his head. "Dominic Shaw." He reached into the back pocket of his jeans. "Taylor wanted me to give this to you. It's the remote device for the front gate. The first button opens the gate. It will close automatically once you drive over the metal plate, but if you want to keep it from closing, then tap on the left."

Sonja took the remote device. "Thank you."

Dom ran a hand over raven-black hair. "I brought up some crates and put them in the library."

She smiled. "Thank you again."

"Taylor's in the back checking the foundation. Do you want me to get him for you?"

"Please don't bother him. I'll see him later."

"I'm going to be in the cellar for most of this morning. So, if you need anything and Taylor's not available, then just come down."

Sonja wanted to tell the man she doubted whether she would need him for anything. He wasn't what she thought of as handsome, but attractive. There were too many sharp angles in his lean face. "Okay."

She walked in the direction of the library, curbing the urge to look over her shoulder to see if Dominic was still staring at her retreating back. There was something about him that was creepy. Taylor had told her that Dom, as he called him, was the only one living on the property, and Sonja deduced that the man had spent so much time alone that he probably resented having to share what had become his private lair. She could not imagine living on a 350-plus-acre property year-round with only sporadic human interaction.

Sonja entered the library. There were eight crates lining one wall. Unfortunately, none of the crates were labeled with their contents, which meant a guessing game as to what she would find. Setting the tote on a small round table, Sonja took out the materials she needed to begin identifying and cataloguing.

"Yes," she said softly after she'd removed the top of the first one. She took out a crystal wineglass protected by Bubble Wrap. Sonja recalled Taylor telling her the late-nineteenth-century mansion was abandoned in the 1960s when the last Bainbridge died at the age of ninety-four, and his father was the last surviving direct descendant of the original owner. She knew bubble wrap hadn't been invented until 1960.

She emptied the crate, lining fragile glassware on an oak Mission-style table. One by one she photographed a liqueur glass with transparent enameling, circa 1900; a Daum Frères cameo glass vase, circa 1890; E. Bakalowits & Söhne floral glasses; four Bohemian drinking glasses with purple and gold medallions on the base and two more Bohemian liqueur glasses in a rich ruby color. The minutes stretched into hours as she took pictures of the glassware, listed them on pads, and then carefully rewrapped them and returned them to the crate. Sonja found it odd that there were no complete sets, leaving her to wonder if someone had packed them away without regard to whether they matched. She marked the crate with the date and its contents, and then moved onto another one.

This one was filled with large flannel bags of velvet boxes she knew contained jewelry. There was a gold, pearl and amethyst brooch; another with parrots bejeweled with diamonds, sapphires, rubies, emeralds and onyx. Her breath caught in her throat when she held a Cartier brooch with large bloodred rubies, diamonds and sapphires. There were more brooches, rings, necklaces, earrings and bracelets with priceless stones set in gold and platinum.

"How's it going, *muñeca*?"

Sonja turned on her chair to find Taylor in the doorway. She smiled at him. "One down and who knows how many more to go."

Pulling over a chair, Taylor sat and brushed a light kiss on her mouth, increasing the pressure until her lips parted. "You look and smell delicious." He didn't think he would ever tire of kissing Sonja, inhaling the sensual fragrance of the perfume that was perfect for her hypnotic feminine scent.

"That's because you're biased," Sonja whispered.

"Hell, yeah." He reached out and picked up a pin with a large blue stone surrounded with gold leaves topped with rubies and stems dotted with diamonds. "Someone really liked bling."

"Someone was really partial to brooches." Sonja handed him one completely covered in diamonds designed with an arrow attached at the back of a heart. "This is an amatory brooch."

"Amatory as in love?"

Sonja nodded. "They were jewels representing sentiment and love, common from the seventeenth to the late nineteenth century. Early symbols included the true lover's knot, and Cupid shooting arrows and flaming hearts like this one."

Taylor set the brooch on the table and picked up a diamond-and-sapphire ring. "This must be worth quite a bit."

Sonja met his eyes. "I've seen enough jewelry to make a rough estimate as to carat weight. The diamond looks to be around two carats and the sapphires flanking the center stone approximately a half carat each, while the platinum setting increases the ring's value exponentially."

Taylor balanced the ring on his palm. "Whoever wore this had a small finger."

Sonja took the ring from him and slipped it on her left hand. "It's a five," she said, taking it off and giving it back to him.

"The diamond is not like any I've ever seen."

"It's known as an Asscher cut."

Taylor peered closely at the ring. "It's exquisite."

"It's beyond exquisite," Sonja agreed. "I'm not going to repack the jewelry. I'll give everything to you for safekeeping until I take them to a gemologist I trust who will give you an honest appraisal."

"You can hold on to them for now."

She blinked slowly. "Are you sure, Taylor?"

"Of course I'm sure. I trust you with my life."

"That's a lot of trusting."

Taylor couldn't pull his gaze away from the large brown eyes with lashes that had touched the ridge of high cheekbones as she slept. "It is for me, because I equate trusting to loving."

A hint of a smile curved the corners of her mouth upward. "And I believe trust is more important than love because people can fall in and out of love. I'd rather trust you than love you."

Sonja had just given Taylor the opening he needed. "Can you love me?"

"I'm sure I can."

Her response was both indifferent and evasive. Do you love me, Sonja?" Taylor saw indecision in her eyes, and that was enough to give him hope that what he felt for her could be reciprocated.

"Why are you asking me this?"

"I'm asking, sweetheart, because I need to know."

Sonja's gaze did not waver as she gave him a long, penetrating stare. "If I tell you that I do, it's not going to change anything between us. Whether you know or admit it, Taylor, you're a traditionalist. You want a wife, two or three kids, a cat and dog, along with a house in the suburbs with the white picket fence."

He struggled not to laugh. "I'm really not crazy about cats."

"I'm serious, Taylor."

"So am I, Sonja. I admit I'm a traditionalist because I don't believe in living with a woman unless I'm married to her."

"That's where we differ, Taylor. I lived with a man to whom I was married, and I realized later that if I'd lived with him I never would've married him."

If she does tell you that she loves you, then don't put any pressure on her to marry. That must be her decision. Taylor recalled his mother's words as if she were whispering in his ear.

"Did you love him, Sonja?"

She closed her eyes and shook her head, and Taylor felt her vulnerability as surely as if it was his own, because falling in love with Sonja Rios-Martin had allowed him to open his heart to love a woman beyond those in his family.

"Good."

"Good?" Sonja repeated.

"Yes. Because he didn't deserve your love."

"And you do?"

"I should hope I do. Remember I told you if we do share a bed, then that decision will have to be yours and yours alone. And it will be the same if you want more."

Sonja rested her head on his shoulder. "Should

I assume you mean living together and then marriage?"

"Yes."

"I need time, Taylor."

"Take all the time you need, sweetheart. You're not going anywhere, and neither am I."

There came a light tapping on the door, and Taylor and Sonja sprang apart. He glanced over his shoulder. "Yes, Dom?"

"Your next interviewee just arrived."

"Thank you, Dom." Pushing back his chair, he stood and rested a hand on Sonja's shoulder. "How long do you plan to hang out here?"

Sonja picked up her cell phone. "I want to leave around three."

"I'll be here much later than that." Robbie had called to say he was coming to New Jersey to spend the weekend with his sister and her family in Hackettstown and wanted to set up a time when they could meet. "I'm going to be tied up for the next few days. Is it all right if I come over Sunday morning to let you sample my chicken and waffles?"

"Of course."

Leaning down, Taylor kissed the bridge of her nose. "I love you."

"Love you back."

"Did I really say that?" Sonja whispered aloud. She did not want to believe she'd admitted to Taylor that she loved him and entertained the possibility of them living together.

She wasn't the twenty-year-old coed with stars in her eyes, and she wouldn't lose her head just because a former top male model and successful engineer had shown an interest in her. At thirty-four, she knew exactly what she wanted and what she would or would not do. In the years following her divorce, Sonja had not had a relationship with a man because she did not trust them not to go from Dr. Jekyll to Mr. Hyde when she least expected. She had dated a few, and those expressing a sincere interest in her were made aware that she wasn't looking for anything serious, and for her *serious* meant sleeping together or seeing each other exclusively.

Taylor said she should take all the time she needed to decide whether they would live together and eventually marry. They had two years, and that was more than enough time for Sonja to know if she'd want to share her life and future with Taylor Williamson.

"I'm sorry to bother you, but is there anything you need, because I'm leaving."

Sonja glanced over her shoulder at Dom. "I don't think so. Thank you for everything."

"Are you coming tomorrow?"

"Yes."

Dom smiled, the expression softening his features to where he appeared almost boyish. "If you need me to move something just send me a text."

"I would if I had your number."

Dom walked into the library, scooped her phone off the table and entered his cell number. "Now you have it."

She returned his smile. "Thank you." Dom left, closing the door behind him, and Sonja shifted her chair to face the door. She didn't want any more walk-in surprises.

Taylor gave his former coworker a rough hug. "You look incredible." Robinson had shaved off his beard and his nut-brown face radiated good health.

"I'm trying, Williamson. Let's go because I'm anxious to see what you're working with."

Taylor unlocked the doors to the Infiniti. "Let's ride, brother."

Twenty-five minutes later, Taylor tapped the remote attached to the visor, and the gates protecting Bainbridge House opened smoothly. The trees lining the path to the property were in full bloom, and dappled sunlight filtered through the foliage like the brilliant diamonds in the priceless jewels that had been packed away for decades. He'd purposely kept busy to keep his mind off Sonja. The interviews had yielded results with positive prospects to fill the positions for his restoration team.

"You've got to be kidding me."

Taylor gave Robbie a sidelong glance. "What's the matter?"

With wide eyes, Robbie stared straight ahead. "Why does this château look as if someone picked it up from the French countryside and set it down in Jersey?"

"That's because someone did, Robbie. I found the

original plans and discovered the château was disassembled stone by stone, stored on ships sailing across the Atlantic, then hauled up here by wagon where it was rebuilt."

"It is magnificent."

Taylor nodded, smiling. "That it is. The interior is even more impressive."

Robbie slowly shook his head. "I can see why you quit working for the firm. I would've done the same if someone left me this place."

"This isn't mine alone. I share the property with my brothers and sister."

"From what I see, you have enough to share with dozens of brothers and sisters."

"What's the expression, Robbie? Too many cooks spoil the broth. Right now it's just me. Two years from now it will be Joaquin, and then Tariq, and finally Viola." Taylor had said *finally* when he wanted to say *hopefully*. "I'm going to take you around the grounds before we go inside."

He led Robbie to the stables and barn. "We have paddocks for six horses."

"Do you plan to house horses on the property?"

"Yes. My brother Tariq is a vet, and his specialty is horses."

"What are you going to do with the barn?" Robbie asked.

Taylor glanced up at the rotting crossbeams. "I'm seriously thinking of demolishing and rebuilding it. There's too much rot. I'd like your expertise when I put up another building."

"What do you plan to use it for?"

"I'm going to need an additional entertainment venue. There are two ballrooms in the main house for weddings and private parties, but after I show you the blueprints, you can suggest how to reconfigure them for meeting rooms and an on-site restaurant. The new structure can be used for larger banquets."

"Where do you plan to rebuild it?" Robbie asked.

"Behind the main house with an enclosed walkway connecting the two structures."

"Will the design conform to the château?"

"Yes. I want it to look as if it is a part of the original design. Will that pose a problem?"

Robbie ran a hand over his shaved pate. "Not at all. But I have to admit it will be my first time designing a château. How large do you want it?"

"Between five- and six-thousand square feet."

Robbie nodded. "That's enough room for almost two hundred people."

"That's sounds about right. Let's go inside and you'll see what awaits you."

Taylor showed Robbie original copies of floor plans and blueprints of the entire property spread out on a banquet table in the larger ballroom. Robbie listened intently when he showed him his blueprint and what he'd planned for the vineyard, orchards, gardens and the golf course. He was forthcoming when voicing reservations about whether to refurbish the golf course.

"I'd keep it, Williamson, because it's only nine holes. If it were eighteen holes then I'd say scrap it.

If you're going to have guests come for a week or even a long weekend, some may want to play a couple of rounds."

Taylor smiled. "True, but if they want to exercise they can always use the health center with a workout room and the indoor pool."

Over the next three hours he showed Robbie the bedroom suites on the second and third floors. He explained the structural modifications he'd planned to make when removing walls and expanding more than half the suites to accommodate four to six guests in each suite. Taylor also told Robbie that he wanted to install two more elevators, bringing the total number to four.

"What do you plan to do with the turrets?"

"I'm still up in the air about the space. I have to confer with my brothers and sister whether they would want live up there or take up residence in the cottages."

"Where do you plan to live?"

"I've claimed one of the cottages."

"Nice, Williamson," Robbie drawled. He extended his hand. "If you want an architectural engineer, then I'm your man."

Taylor shook the proffered hand. "Thanks for joining the team." He had his two architectural experts: Sonja Rios-Martin and Robinson Harris.

Chapter Fourteen

Taylor brushed a kiss over Sonja's mouth when she opened the door. As promised, he'd planned to make chicken and waffles for their first Sunday brunch. "Hey, beautiful."

She flushed with the compliment. "Hey yourself, handsome."

He'd stopped by the night before and left a container of marinating chicken. He did not ask to stay over and for that Sonja was grateful. She wasn't quite ready to take their relationship to the next level. After all, they had two years in which to get to know each other in and out of bed.

Not having dinner together for several days had allowed her more time to devote to the contents of the trunks. She had anticipated spending hours on the project so she'd planned slow cooker meals. Beef stew and chili accompanied with salad fortified her for lunch and dinner.

"I've set out the cast-iron pot and waffle iron for you."

"Good." Taylor held up a small shopping bag. "I have all I need in here to make red velvet waffles."

Sonja moaned, smiling. "I am addicted to anything red velvet."

Taylor winked at her. "And I'm addicted to what I'm looking at."

She waved at him. "Flattery will get you nowhere."

"It's not flattery, *muñeca*. It is the truth."

Sonja looped her arm through his free one. "Come and feed me. I'm starved."

Hours later, Sonja reclined against Taylor on the sofa in the family room, her back resting against his chest. "I have a confession to make."

He pressed a kiss on her hair. "And that is?"

"You were right about your chicken and waffles. They were the best I've ever eaten." The chicken, drizzled with melted butter and honey, was the perfect complement to the fluffy red-hued Belgian waffles. They'd opted for freshly squeezed orange juice sans champagne as an accompanying beverage.

"Does this mean we can do this again?"

Tilting her chin, she smiled up at him staring

down at her. "Yes. We can do this again and again for a long time to come."

"How long, darling?"

"For a very long time, *papi*. I've spent the past three days thinking about what we talked about in the château's library. You are so different from Hugh that it's frightening, and that's why I wouldn't allow myself to get close to you. But, in spite of that, I couldn't help falling in love with you."

"Or I you, Sonja," he whispered. "You just don't know how easy it is to love you."

Sonja closed her eyes, realizing that what she was about to tell Taylor would change her, change them forever. "I want to know what love is, Taylor. I need you to make love to me."

Sonja remembered Taylor carrying her out of the family room and up the staircase to her bedroom. He took his time undressing her and then himself. She closed her eyes after he'd slipped on a condom and before she welcomed him into her embrace for their introductory dance of shared passion.

She bit her lower lip to stop the moans of pleasure rippling through her body like currents of electricity, shocking every nerve ending as she experienced la petite mort for the first time in her life. The orgasms kept coming, overlapping one another until Sonja feared fainting.

"I love you. I love you," she repeated over and over until it'd become a litany. "I love you, Taylor Edward Williamson, and I will marry you and have your babies."

* * *

Taylor thought he was hallucinating. Passion had clouded his mind to the point that he did not know where he began or ended.

"When, babe?"

Sonja rubbed her leg over the back of his. "Christmas. I want a Christmas wedding at Bainbridge House in the small ballroom with just friends and family in attendance."

"My mother can't be there because she'll still be on her cruise."

"Then it will have to be the following Christmas."

Taylor supported his greater weight on his forearms as he loathed pulling out of her body. "Are you sure? We could marry before she leaves for her cruise in August."

"No, Taylor. I want to wait. There's no need for us to rush anything. Didn't you say you're not going anywhere?"

"Yes, I did."

"I'm also not going anywhere. I'm going to be here today, tomorrow and all the days thereafter. And the day I marry you I want us to start baby making. Meanwhile I'm going to go on birth control because I don't want to become a baby mama before we're married."

Taylor wanted to tell Sonja he had no intention of fathering a child and deserting her, married or not. He did not want to repeat the scenario of his biological parents' fractured relationship.

"I will protect you until then."

He pulled out, left the bed and went into the bathroom to discard the condom. Sonja wanted to marry the following Christmas, and that meant an eighteenth-month engagement. By that time, the extension to the château would be completed and they could hold the ceremony and reception there. Taylor returned to the bedroom and got into bed beside Sonja, who'd turned on her side. She moaned softly when he pressed his groin against her rounded hips. Resting his arm over her waist, Taylor pulled her even closer. His breathing slowed until he fell into a slumber reserved for sated lovers.

Sonja felt as if she was existing in an alternative universe as spring gave way to summer. She and Taylor were now living together. His mother had finally sold the house where she'd raised her children and moved into her condo. Days later, she flew out to the West Coast for a reunion of her college sorority sisters, and Taylor packed up his clothes and stored them in the closet in the smaller bedroom.

She went to Bainbridge House on Mondays, Wednesdays and Fridays, and worked from home on Tuesday and Thursdays. Cloistered behind the door in the château's library she heard but rarely saw the workmen going about their tasks. Pickup trucks and vans lined the driveway, and several dumpsters were positioned around the house.

Her condo's backyard had undergone a metamorphosis with all-weather furniture, umbrellas, portable lighting, a gas grill and fire pit, and Sonja found herself, weather permitting, eating breakfast and dinner outdoors. She and Taylor grilled chicken, steak, fish, veggies, and fruit, leaving little or no cleanup in the kitchen.

She was halfway through emptying one trunk when she found a batch of letters wrapped with a red ribbon and finally discovered who MS was. Melanie Shaw had been Charles Bainbridge's mistress, and also a house servant and the mother of his love child. Why, she mused, were a mistress's love letters stored with possessions where anyone might discover them?

"Oh, my word," she gasped when realization dawned. The property's caretaker was a Shaw, and Sonja wondered if there was connection between Melanie and Dominic. She did not want to invade his privacy, yet the historian in her wanted and needed to uncover the truth.

Reaching for her cell phone, she sent Dom a text asking if she could talk to him. She didn't have to wait for his reply, and he said he would available later that afternoon to meet in the library.

Taylor walked in the direction of the small ballroom that he'd set up as a temporary office and stopped when he heard Sonja's voice coming from the library. The door was slightly ajar, and he was caught completely off guard when he saw Sonja in Dom's arms. Not only wasn't it her scheduled day to work outside the condo, but he hadn't expected to see her embracing the caretaker.

Taking long strides, he made his way to the ballroom and closed the pocket doors as scalding fury gripped him and he struggled to draw a normal breath. Taylor did not want to believe the woman with whom he'd fallen in love, slept beside every night and made love to was having an affair with another man. When she came in on Mondays, Wednesdays and Fridays he rarely saw her because she tended to work behind closed doors. However, he was aware that after she'd completed several crates Dom would return them to the cellar and bring up more.

He paced the length of the ballroom, pounding his fist into his hand when he'd wanted to punch something hard to make him forget about the emotional pain threatening to explode into unrestrained anger. Taylor sat on the stool near the drafting table, staring at the plans he and Robbie had designed on the computer and revised several times before they were finalized and printed. He lost track of time, then stood and walked out of the ballroom to talk to Dom.

He saw Dom kneeling near a flower bed, pulling out weeds. "We need to talk."

Dom rose and met his eyes. "What about?"

"I want you to stay away from Sonja."

The green eyes narrowed like a cat ready to attack. "What the hell are you talking about?"

Taylor chose his words carefully. "I don't want you anywhere around her when she's working in the library. Meanwhile, I'll have someone else move the crates."

Dom crossed his arms over his chest in a gesture mirroring defiance. "Have you forgotten that you're not my boss? You don't pay my salary, therefore I don't have to take orders from you. But if you want me to stay away from Sonja, then I will. Not because you say so, but because I don't want to make trouble for her." Turning on his heel, he walked away, leaving Taylor staring at his back.

Taylor cursed to himself—raw, ugly, frustrated curses because Dom was right. He wasn't his boss, and it wasn't incumbent upon him to pay the man's wages, therefore he couldn't fire him. However, he did pay Sonja; he decided to wait until later to confront her.

Sonja couldn't believe what she was hearing. The man she'd pledged her future to had accused her of cheating on him with another man. It was history repeating itself. "You saw something you probably shouldn't have seen and jumped to the conclusion that I was seeing another man. Maybe you should have come into the library instead of accusing an innocent man. What happened to trust, Taylor!" She was screaming but no longer cared. "Remember I told you that I value trust over love? I believed once we agreed to live and sleep together that we would trust each other." She threw up both hands. "You're no different from Hugh because he, too, didn't trust me." The tears she'd held at bay fell, and she backed away when Taylor attempted to touch her. "Don't! I have to get away. Even if it is just for a few days." She swiped angrily at the tears streaming down her face and walked over to the closet to take out a suitcase.

"Where are you going, Sonja?"

"I don't know. I'll find out when I get there."

There weren't that many places she could go aside from her parents', and her aunt and uncle's. She thought about Viola and quickly changed her mind. Taylor was her brother, and there was no doubt she would side with him.

She opened drawers and threw clothes in haphazardly before going into the bathroom to gather a number of personal items and products. Sonja closed the bag, grabbed her tote off the chair and went downstairs. She didn't know if Taylor was following her as she opened the door and walked out into the late-afternoon warmth. It wasn't until she'd left the complex that she decided to drive to her parents' house and spend time there to clear her head.

Sonja knew they were away, but she had the keys and the code to the house's security system. It was almost laughable. When she left Hugh she'd run to her mother. And now she was doing it again. There was something about sitting on the porch and staring at the lake that she found therapeutic. She planned to spend the weekend there, and when she returned she would continue with her project. Once it ended she would move on to the next one.

* * *

Taylor sat in the family room staring at the flickering images on the flat screen. Night had fallen and he hadn't turned on any lights. If it hadn't been for the sound of the television the house would've been as quiet as a tomb. He'd blown it. Jealousy had reared its ugly head, and he'd accused the woman he loved passionately of sleeping with another man. It had taken her almost two minutes to reply to his accusation, and during that time he'd felt triumphant because she hadn't thought he knew. His victory was short-lived when she told him there was nothing going on between her and Dominic, and what he'd witnessed was a friendly hug between friends. It was when she told him he was the same as her ex-husband that it was apparent he'd done something that made her distrust him. Taylor decided to give Sonja a few days to cool off before calling her. After all, she hadn't put enough clothes in the bag to last more than that.

Taylor counted off the days: Wednesday, Thursday, Friday and Saturday. It was now Sunday and Sonja hadn't come back or returned any of his calls, but he didn't want to believe he'd lost her. His apprehension increased knowing it wasn't the first time she'd walked away from a relationship.

He'd become a detective when he accessed the credit card he'd given her and discovered she hadn't used it for gas, food or lodging. He thought about calling her uncle before realizing that wasn't a good idea. If Nelson didn't know where she was and he had to explain what had happened, the situation could possibly turn hostile between him and the retired police officer.

Taking the cell phone off the bedside table, he called the one person he could talk to without prejudice. "What's up, Taylor?"

"You don't want to know, Viola."

"What's the matter?"

He registered the apprehension in his sister's voice. "I need to talk to you about Sonja."

"What did you do to her?"

"Is she there with you?"

"No. I spoke to her a couple of days ago to let her know I'm planning to leave The Cellar at the end of the summer and then hang out with you until the mansion's kitchen is up and running."

The news rendered Taylor speechless. "When were you going to tell me?" he asked, recovering his voice.

"I just told you."

"Stop playing games."

"And don't take that tone with me, Taylor Williamson. I am not responsible for what went down between you and Sonja."

Taylor knew he had to tell his sister about his relationship with her friend; he had no one else to talk to. "We had a disagreement and she left, and I haven't seen or heard from her since Thursday."

"What did you do to her?"

"It wasn't what I did but what I said."

"Tell me everything, Taylor, and don't leave anything out."

Taylor was forthcoming when he told his sister about his relationship with Sonja and their agreement to live together and the importance of trust. "I violated that trust when I saw her with another man and accused her of being unfaithful. That's when she told me I was just like her ex-husband."

"She's right, Taylor. The only difference is your ages. Her ex was more than twenty years older than Sonja and a predator. He loved younger women, and as a college professor he preyed on his female students. Sonja told me he was handsome, charming and erudite, and she fell hard for him. When he noticed younger men staring at her he suspected she was flirting with them. The one time he spotted her hugging one of his male students he went into a jealous rage and accused her of sleeping with the innocent boy. She denied it, and he begged her to forgive him and that it would never happen again. But it did happen again over and over, and that's when Sonja knew she'd made a mistake marrying Hugh Davies.

"She moved out of their bedroom and refused to host his parties. He turned on her. He placed a tracking device on her car and stopped giving her money. She looked so ashamed, Taylor, when she admitted to me that she'd begun stealing from her husband whenever he put down his wallet. Two dollars here and five dollars at another time. After a while she had enough money to buy a prepaid phone and hid it where she knew he would never find it.

"Then the monster made her a prisoner in her own home after he changed the locks on the doors in the house and refused to give her a set of keys. It was a double cylinder lock where you needed a key to unlock the door from the inside to get out. She waited two months before she began pilfering again. This time it was tens and twenties because she was planning to escape. She gave the SOB four years of her life because she'd hoped it would get better, but it never got better.

"There were times when she wanted to call her father to tell him what she had been going through but knew he would've murdered Hugh. She finally was able to escape after she found a second set of keys. She walked away when he went out of town for a conference. She never asked her husband to love her. All she wanted was for him to trust her. I was the only one who knew what her ex did to her, and now you know."

Taylor felt an icy shiver eddy down his back as if doused by cold water. Sonja had told him about feeling smothered but hadn't given him any details of what she'd endured with her ex-husband. Now he knew why she'd insisted he trust her. "I'm sorry, Viola."

"Don't tell me, Taylor! Tell your girlfriend."

"I've called and left voice mail messages for her to call me. She hasn't returned any of them."

"I'm going to do this one favor for you, brother, and if you mess it up then you're on your own. I'm going to call her and let her know I've spoken to you. I'm also going to tell her to send you a text to let you know she's safe. And you're going to text her back that you're willing to give her as much time as she needs to get her head straight. That can be either two days, two weeks or even two months. I'm warning you, Taylor. If you put pressure on her to come back, you *will* lose her—for good."

"Okay, Viola."

"Say it like you mean it, Taylor."

"I promise not to put any pressure on her."

"That's better, brother love. I'll talk to you at another time about why I've decided to become executive chef for Bainbridge House."

"Thank you, baby sis."

"You're welcome. I'm on vacation for the next two weeks, so if you need a shoulder I'll rent a car, drive up and hang out with you."

Taylor smiled for the first time in days. "I'd like that. We've just begun working on the house and I'd like to show you the plans for the restoration."

"That's a bet. I'll contact you before I come. Now hang up so I can call my friend."

Taylor ended the call and pressed his head against a mound of pillows under his back and shoulders. His conversation with Viola had left him shaken.

He could not imagine a young woman becoming so intimidated that she feared telling her parents that her husband had made her a virtual prisoner in her own home.

It was like a rerun with Sonja and Dom. He'd asked the caretaker to stay away from Sonja. However, it was obvious Dom had misconstrued it as a threat, not a request. Taylor hadn't said anything to Sonja once he'd noticed Dom lingering outside the library waiting for her to open the door. It wasn't until he spied them embracing that he began to wonder if it wasn't the first time Sonja and Dom had been together whenever the door was closed. He sucked in a lungful of air and held it for several seconds before he exhaled an audible sigh. Viola had asked him to wait and he would.

Sonja was sitting on a rocker on the porch, enjoying her second cup of coffee, when her cell phone rang. Taylor had left several voice mail messages asking her to call him. She wasn't ready to listen to anything he had to say. And she was going through her own self-examination once she realized she'd waited almost ten years to become involved with a man who had the same personality trait as the one she'd married: distrust.

The phone continued to ring and when she reached over to silence it she saw the name and number on the screen. The caller wasn't Taylor.

"Hi, Viola."

"How are you doing?"

Sonja smiled. "I'm better."

"Good. I'm calling to let you know I spoke to my brother. I don't want you to bite my head off, but I had to tell him everything you'd gone through with your ex-husband."

Sonja closed her eyes. "It's okay, Viola. It doesn't matter anymore."

"Yes, it does matter because my brother is in love with you. I'm not going to interfere any more, but I want you to text him that you're okay. Will you please do that for me?"

"Yes, Viola."

"Yes, what?"

"I'll text him." Sonja stared at the calm surface of the lake. "I love Taylor."

"You love Taylor, and he loves you. As two mature adults you should be able to work through your differences because I've always wanted a sister."

Sonja shook her head, smiling. "What you want is a sister-in-law."

"That, too," Viola drawled. "Since graduating culinary school, I've always wanted to run my own kitchen and prepare a wedding banquet. That definitely can become a reality if you marry my brother at Bainbridge House."

Sonja wanted to tell her friend that wasn't going to happen. Not when the man she had fallen for did not trust her to be a faithful wife. "I'm going to text Taylor to let him know I'm okay," she said instead.

"I'm not going to ask where you are, because if Taylor asks me I don't want to lie to him. When are you going back?"

"Probably in a couple of days. Originally I'd planned to spend the weekend here, but when I got up this morning I knew I needed more time to get my head together." What she didn't tell her friend was that she had to decide whether to move out of the condo, lease a car in her name and find a rental within the vicinity of Bainbridge House or stay where she was. She had no intention of living with Taylor after their breakup.

"Good. I'll call you again in a couple of days."

"Okay, Viola." Sonja ended the call and sent a text to Taylor.

Viola: I'm okay. Need some time to myself. Will be in touch.

She did not have to wait for his reply.

Taylor: Take all the time you need. I'll be here if or when you decide to come back.

If or when. The three words were branded into her head. Had he believed she would walk away from her work? That she was so unprofessional that she would abandon a project she'd sought since becoming an architectural historian? Bainbridge House wasn't just a structure some celebrity had erected because they were obsessed with all things French. Not only was it listed on National Register of Historic Places, it was originally commissioned in 1803 by a French nobleman who had fled to France during the Haitian Revolution as a gift to his new bride. And it wasn't until 1883 that Charles Bainbridge spotted the château and offered to purchase it from the then-impoverished owners who were hard-pressed to make the necessary repairs to the mansion. The Bainbridge House had an illustrious history, and Sonja wanted her name included in the restoration narrative once she listed it on her résumé. And she would follow Taylor's advice and take the time needed to sort out the next phase of her life.

Sonja was still at the lake house when her parents returned two weeks later, and she told them she was on holiday and needed a place to stay because she'd been working nonstop on the project. She knew her mother didn't believe her when she motioned with her head that they should go outside where James Martin couldn't overhear their conversation.

Rather than sit, she suggested they walk. Then Sonja told her mother everything from the time she'd gone out with Hugh for the first time, what he'd accused her of and why she'd had to plan her escape. She felt as if she'd been stabbed in the heart when she saw Maria cry.

"Why didn't you say something, *chica*?"

Sonja bit her lip in attempt not to lose her composure. It had been a long time since her mother had called her *little girl*, and in that instant she felt like an innocent, trusting little girl who had surrendered her will to someone so undeserving. "I didn't say anything because I didn't want Dad to kill him. And you know your husband would've done it, Mami."

"No, he wouldn't. He would've told your brother to get one of his buddies to take him out and make it look like an accident."

"See! That's why I didn't say anything."

"I know you didn't come here because of your psycho ex. Should I assume you've fallen in love with someone and you need your mama's advice as to how to proceed?"

"How did you know?"

Maria shook her head. "I don't know why kids believe their parents are oblivious. The last time we spoke I could hear something in your voice that told me you were happy, and that joy had come from you being in love. When you didn't tell me who he was I decided not to pry. But that was then, and this is now because I want to know everything."

Sonja was forthcoming about her relationship with Taylor. She admitted she was in love with him and wanted to marry him, yet that wasn't possible if he did not trust her.

They stopped in front of a boathouse and Maria turned to face her. "Can you put yourself in his situation and imagine you saw him hugging another woman. Wouldn't your first impulse be to accuse him of cheating on you?"

Sonja stomped her foot. "Why are you taking his side?"

Maria glared at her. "I'm not taking sides, Sonja. I

just want you to think about what this man has done for you. You claim he doesn't want to live with a woman unless he is married to her, yet he's done just that. Did you ask him why? There must be good reason why he doesn't believe in shacking up. The man appears to be everything that good-for-nothing you married wasn't for you to walk away without listening to him. He's jealous because he loves you, *chica*. And you've told me he's willing to give you all the time you need to get your head together."

Sonja nodded. "Yes."

"How long have you been here?"

"A little more than two weeks."

"That's more than enough time. Now, when we get back to the house I want you to pack your stuff and be ready to leave in the morning."

"Mami!"

"Don't Mami me, Sonja Mariana Rios-Martin! You're a thirty-four-year-old woman not a little girl running to her parents when things don't work out the way you want. Then you must ask yourself when you need to stop running and deal with your problems head-on. Your Taylor may not be perfect, but neither are you."

"What went on between me and Dominic was innocent, Mami. He'd disclosed something to me that I'd promised never to tell anyone, and he'd hugged me in appreciation."

"Wouldn't a handshake have been better?"

"I suppose it would, but what's done can't be undone."

"What's going to be done is you leaving my house tomorrow morning and going back to Jersey to handle your business."

Sonja knew by Maria's expression and tone that she was serious about her not staying. "Okay. I'll leave in the morning."

Chapter Fifteen

Taylor waited for the arm to go up to drive into the gated community. It had been more than two weeks since Sonja left, and he hadn't realized how much he missed her until it was time for him to come home. As promised, Viola had driven up to spend two days with him, and it was the distraction he'd needed not to dwell on Sonja.

Viola had toured the kitchen, jotting down notes as to what she needed to update the space. She hadn't told anyone she was leaving The Cellar in mid-September and vacating her Greenwich Village apartment at the same time. She'd planned to move back to New Jersey and stay in their mother's condo while Elise was away. His sister did not bring up the topic of Sonja and for that he was grateful.

His foot hit the brake hard, causing the SUV to screech to a stop when he spied Sonja's vehicle parked in the driveway. Taylor wondered if she'd come back to pick up the rest of her clothes because she always parked in the garage.

Maneuvering in behind her car, he got out and opened the outer door. He smiled. Sonja always left that door unlocked to save him having to open two. He unlocked the inner one and walked in. Then he saw her. She looked the same, yet there was something different about her, and it wasn't only the curly hair falling over her shoulders. And it wasn't that she'd lost weight. It was her eyes when she stared at him.

"Hello, Sonja."

Her impassive expression did not change. "Hello, Taylor."

"Why didn't you tell me you were coming back?"

She blinked once. "I wanted to surprise you."

"I must say I am shocked and surprised."

"We have to talk."

Taylor did not want to believe they were talking to each other like strangers. "Okay. Have you eaten?"

"No."

"Then we'll talk in the kitchen while I put something together."

Taylor tossed his keys in a straw basket on the table in the entryway. He waited for Sonja to precede him and then followed her into the kitchen. She sat at the breakfast bar as he washed his hands in the half bath off the kitchen. He stared at his reflection in the mirror over the sink. He hadn't shaved in over a week, and there were tiny gray hairs in the stubble.

He returned to the kitchen and opened the fridge. "I made meat loaf using your recipe, so I hope you don't mind eating leftovers. I'll bake some potatoes and put together a salad to go with it."

Sonja wanted to scream at Taylor to stop, stop acting as if she was someone he'd met a few days ago and didn't know what she'd like. "I don't mind. What I do mind is you being overly polite and acting as if you don't know what I like to eat."

Taylor rested both hands, palms down, on the countertop. "I've been trying to be polite and patient while you got, as you said, your head together. Well, my head is totally together, and I want and need to know what you want from me."

Sonja closed her eyes and sighed. "I need you to be honest with me, Taylor."

"What about trust, Sonja? Weren't you the one who declared that trust is more important than love, or maybe even honesty?"

"Yes. And I'm being honest when I tell you that nothing happened between me and Dominic. I went to Bainbridge House to ask him about something I'd discovered in one of the trunks. He told me what I needed to know, and then made me promise never to tell anyone. It's when I promised him his secret was safe with me that he hugged me. End of story.

It had been more than ten years since I'd allowed a man to touch my body or make love to me because I didn't trust them not to go from Dr. Jekyll to Mr. Hyde. You were that man, Taylor, and when you accused me of cheating on you with Dominic it was as if I were reliving what I'd gone through with my ex. He accused me of sleeping with any and every man that glanced at me, so many that I lost count after the four or fifth one. And that was something I did not want to experience with you."

Taylor rounded the bar and eased her off the stool. "I'm so sorry, darling. I've been a fool and it was only after you'd left me, and Viola told me what you'd gone through with your ex that I had to apologize to Dom."

With wide eyes, Sonja stared at him not daring to believe what she'd just heard. "You approached him about me?"

"I did."

"To tell him to stay away from you."

"You didn't!"

"Yes, I did because I was jealous, Sonja. And angry. I saw how he'd linger outside the library door, waiting for you to open it."

"You're a fool, Taylor. I'd text him to come and pick up a crate I'd finished to take back to the cellar. He'd wait until I opened the door to come in. It was more than I could say for you when you'd walk in without bothering to knock and lock the door behind you."

She turned her head to hide a smile when his expression became sheepish. It was during those times when he'd come in to massage her back and shoulders and they'd end up kissing and touching each other, stopping short of making love.

Taylor rested his hands on her shoulders. "You enjoyed those impromptu visits as much as I did."

"I did. What did Dominic say when you accused him of fooling around with me?"

"He told me in no uncertain words that I wasn't his boss and couldn't tell him what to do. But he did promise to stay away from you because he didn't want to cause any trouble between us."

"Wouldn't it have been easier to tell him that I'm your fiancée?"

"But you weren't, Sonja. I know we talked about marriage, but we hadn't made a formal announcement."

"You're right about that. Maybe if I'd been wearing an engagement ring Dominic would've reacted differently to my agreeing to keep his promise."

Taylor's hand went to her waist, pulling her close. "I'm so sorry for not trusting you. Will you forgive me?"

"I'll think about it." Sonja wasn't going to let him off that easily.

"You said you wanted honesty, and I'm going to tell you something about myself because I love you and want to spend the rest of my life with you."

"Is it something most people don't know about?"

He nodded. "Yes."

Sonja cradled his face, her eyes making love to

it. Talking with her mother had made her look at life differently, that as a thirtysomething woman she couldn't continue to run away when she had to stand and work out her problems. Spending time away from Taylor had made her realize how much she loved and missed him, and the next time he proposed marriage she would give him a resounding yes without any attached stipulations.

"What's said in this house will remain in this house."

She rested her forehead against his chest, holding back tears when he told her he never knew the man that fathered him because he'd deserted his mother when she told him she was carrying his child. And he didn't remember his mother, who'd died from kidney disease when he was three. He had gone to live with an aunt who neglected him, and it wasn't until he'd entered the first grade that the school social worker intervened and he was placed in the home of Conrad and Elise Williamson as their first foster child.

"It took a while to adjust to wearing clean clothes, sleeping in my own bed, having enough to eat and calling a woman that looked nothing like me Mom. It took me a while to trust her when she said I could live with her for as long as I wanted. That's when I told her I never wanted to leave, and I would always be her son. She was able to convince Conrad to apply for more foster children, and that's how I ended up with a sister and three brothers. The day we were all legally adopted we promised one another not tell folks we weren't biological brothers and sister even though we don't all look alike."

Tilting her chin, Sonja smiled up at Taylor. "Your parents were truly remarkable people."

"My Dad was, and mother is," he said proudly.

"And they raised a remarkable son and daughter."

"My other three brothers are also remarkable."

"I can't wait to meet them."

Taylor's inky-black eyebrows lifted. "Are you saying you want to join my remarkable family?"

Sonja couldn't help smiling because she was so happy she feared her heart would burst. "If it means becoming your wife, then my answer is yes." Tightening his grip on her waist, Taylor lifted her off her feet and kissed her until she struggled to breathe. "Taylor, stop before I pass out."

"Now that we're engaged, you need a ring. I'm going upstairs to look at your jewelry stash to see if I can find one Conrad Williamson would want to pass along to his future daughter-in-law."

Sonja sat on the stool, waiting for Taylor to return. She'd brought all the jewelry home and stored it in a portable safe in the closet in the spare bedroom until it could be appraised. She estimated the rings, bracelets, necklaces, brooches, watches, hair and tie clips were worth millions and told Taylor he should confer with his mother and siblings which estate pieces they wanted to keep or sell.

Sonja covered her mouth with her right hand when Taylor returned holding the Asscher diamond ring between his thumb and forefinger. Her eyes widened when he went down on one knee and grasped her left hand.

"Miss Sonja Rios-Martin, will you do me the honor of becoming my wife?"

She had accused of him being traditional and he was playing the part. "Yes, Mr. Taylor Edward Williamson, I will marry you."

Taylor slipped the priceless ring on her finger, rose and kissed her mouth. "Thank you, *muñeca*. And thank you for trusting me enough to accept me as your future husband."

"I love you for being you and for trusting me with your family's secret."

He eased back, meeting her eyes. "You have no idea how much I love you, Sonja."

"I think I do," she said shyly when she saw lust shimmering in the dark eyes. "Dinner will have wait until you show me, *papi*."

Taylor scooped her off the stool, took the stairs two at a time and walked into the bedroom. No words were spoken because their bodies communicated wordlessly how much they had come to love each other. They fell asleep, their limbs entwined, and it was much later when they left the bed to shower together before returning to the kitchen to eat and make plans for their future and establish a new foundation for Bainbridge House.

* * * * *

Don't miss the next Bainbridge House novel,
publishing later in 2021!

And in the meantime, check out these other
great fresh start romances:

The Trouble with Picket Fences
by Teri Wilson

She Dreamed of a Cowboy
by Joanna Sims

His Forever Texas Rose
by Stella Bagwell

Available now wherever
Harlequin Special Edition books
and ebooks are sold!

*Nissa Lang knows Desmond Stilling is out of her league.
He's a CEO, she's a teacher. He's gorgeous, she's…
not. So when her house-sitting gig falls through and
Desmond offers her a place to stay for the summer, she
vows not to reveal how she's felt about him since their
first—and only—kiss.*

Read on for a sneak peek at
Before Summer Ends,
by #1 New York Times *bestselling author*
Susan Mallery.

"You're welcome to join me if you'd like. Unless you have plans. It's Saturday, after all."

Plans as in a date? Yeah, not so much these days. In fact, she hadn't been in a serious relationship since she and James had broken up over two years ago.

"I don't date," she blurted before she could stop herself. "I mean, I can, but I don't. Or I haven't been. Um, lately."

She consciously pressed her lips together to stop herself from babbling like an idiot, despite the fact that the damage was done.

"So, dinner?" Desmond asked, rescuing her without commenting on her babbling.

"I'd like that. After I shower. Meet back down here in half an hour?"

"Perfect."

There was an awkward moment when they both tried to go through the kitchen door at the same time. Desmond stepped back and waved her in front of him. She hurried out, then raced up the stairs and practically ran for her bedroom. Once there, she closed the door and leaned against it.

"Talking isn't hard," she whispered to herself. "You've been doing it since you were two. You know how to do this."

But when it came to being around Desmond, knowing and doing were two different things.

Don't miss
Before Summer Ends *by Susan Mallery,*
available May 2021 wherever
Harlequin Special Edition books and ebooks are sold.

Harlequin.com

Get 4 FREE REWARDS!

We'll send you 2 FREE Books plus 2 FREE Mystery Gifts.

Harlequin Special Edition books relate to finding comfort and strength in the support of loved ones and enjoying the journey no matter what life throws your way.

FREE
Value Over
$20
